I0727122

Unholy Blood

Ian Gielen

Copyright ©, Ian Gielen, 2025

All rights reserved. No parts of this book may be copied, distributed, or published in any form without permission from the publisher. For permissions contact: Ian.Gielen@gmail.com.

This is a work of fiction in which all events and characters in this book are completely imaginary. Any resemblance to actual people is entirely coincidental.

ISBN: 978-1-7640126-1-4
Cover designed by Adrian Medina
Edited by Stephanie Huddle
Formatted by Jyl Glenn
Published by Ian Gielen

For all those who are hesitant to follow their dreams, believing they are nothing more than fleeting whispers in the dark. Let self-doubt no longer bind you. Break the chains, step forward and bring those dreams into the light.

"Hell is empty, and all the devils are here." — William Shakespeare, The Tempest

PROLOGUE

In the obsidian heart of an ancient labyrinthine cave, where shadows reign and weave their intricate tapestries, an ecosystem untouched by human hands thrives. Creatures large and small slither, crawl, slide, fly, and swim their way through the purity of their home, long since explored by all. The age-long predator and prey dance familiar and expected by all beings living there plays out as creatures succumb to their biological needs.

One cavern stands apart in the secluded twists and turns of the cave system, one that all but a single species of creature dares to live. It's this cavern that suddenly explodes with the sounds of agitated trills, filling the vast space with noise it hadn't experienced in any living being's lifetime that existed there. All except for one.

In a secluded corner of the cavern, where few but the most unfortunate of the flying creatures dared to go, something stirred. Its distended, ridged ears flick in annoyance, the cacophony of sound rousing it from its decades-long dormancy. With a flutter, its eyelids open slowly, disturbing dust and dirt particles that had built up over time. The protective, nictitating membrane retracts from eyes that instantly pierce the velvety darkness of its surroundings. Its eyes glow with bioluminescence as its vision unfolds like a hidden tapestry. The cave is alight with sound, the high-pitched squeaks of its smaller cousins that bounce off the walls creating a detailed sonic map of the cavern.

It shifts slowly, its ancient leathery skin crackling and groaning with movement it hadn't experienced in decades. Despite the arcane symphony of the sound filling the cavern, it senses something it hadn't detected since it was last active. Before its stomach, now down to its last reserve of sustenance, was filled with the freshness of its preferred meat. The meat that was both achingly familiar to it and that it craved. But the time for hunting was not yet nigh. Soon. In times past, it hadn't been hard to find its prey, as dangerous as it sometimes was to hunt. It knew it would be the same the next time it awoke. It closed its eyes once more and sank back into its dormancy, leaving the cavern to the anxious and yearning cries of its brethren.

Chapter One
Jack: 26th October

"Ahhhhh! Fuck!" Mason cried out as he teetered precariously on the edge of the small outcropping of rock overlooking a ravine. Stones and shards of scree loosened by his footsteps tumbled down the small slope as Mason windmilled his arms frantically, trying to keep his balance.

"You fucking idiot," Jack said with an outlandish laugh that filled the valley as he grabbed hold of one of Mason's arms and hauled him back.

"You should know by now not to walk so close to the edge. How many years have we been hiking now, and yet you're still doing it?"

"Yeah, well, gotta have some excitement in your life, you know?" Mason muttered, taking in some quick breaths to calm his pounding heart.

"One of these days, I won't be quick enough to save your sorry ass," Jack said with a grin.

He crouched down, placing his backpack on the ground, and rummaged through its front pocket, pulling out a crumpled map. Its dog-eared corners and rips in its surface told the tale of its overuse. His finger traced a line from the Coon Mountain trail to a point well off it near the base of Coon Mountain where they were now. Checking his watch, he judged they had about another hour left before they had to head back to meet the trail. Travelling in near darkness in unfamiliar terrain was never a good idea.

As an experienced hiker, Jack had never relied on a compass. As inadvisable as that was, he instead relied on his sense of direction. A sense that had never let him down yet. He cast a quick look at Mason, who was leaning back against the jagged mountainside behind him, still taking in gulps of breath.

He smiled again and shook his head. Mason, on the other hand, would get lost at the slightest deviation off course. Almost as experienced as he was, Mason had never had a good sense of direction; instead, he relied on others to lead the way. He never once had gone hiking without someone with him, and that someone was usually Jack.

Even away from college football, Jack noted their relationship was much the same. Both hailing from Syracuse University, the pair were a part of the Syracuse Orange football team. On the field, Jack, the quarterback, directed the plays, and Mason, the left tackle, was his constant defender, a role that reflected their friendship. At least on the field, Mason couldn't get lost. Jack chuckled softly to himself.

"When you're ready to stop gulping air like some demented fish, we should get a move on."

Mason grinned in reply and stuck his middle finger up at him.

Jack surveyed the landscape ahead of them. After branching off the well-trodden path of the Coon Mountain trail that wove between the trees, Jack had decided to explore and follow the base of the cliffs as they meandered downward. Mostly parallel to the path, it should have been easy going despite the rough terrain until Mason had somehow managed to find the edge of a particularly steep slope to almost fall off of.

The landscape ahead of them continued to dip, spiralling outward in a U-shaped formation away from the path. Trees were sparse in this area, replaced instead by large boulders and rocks that had come loose from the mountains over time. Moss covered some of the older boulders whilst wildflowers and ferns provided a splash of colour amongst the otherwise dull bone-white of the landscape. In the far corner, at the apex of the U-curve, there looked to be some vines covering a section of the cliff. If they left now, they would have just enough time to follow the curve of the mountains before they had to head back to the trail.

The pair set off once more, Mason this time taking extra care placing his feet, which slowed their pace down significantly.

"Take your time, why don't ya," Jack called back over his shoulder, noticing how far Mason was lagging behind.

"Yeah, well, you didn't almost break your neck falling off a cliff," Mason retorted sarcastically.

"Bro, it would have been a broken ankle at the worst. Don't be such a wuss."

"Did you forget we play the second-ranked team this weekend? No way I want to break anything right now."

"Yeah, yeah," Jack said, waving him off with a laugh. "You know I do all the work anyway," Jack called back, throwing him a grin.

"Bullshit, without me you wouldn't get half the throws in that you do," Mason said, giving him another finger.

Mason had him there. He was always the first to defend

Jack and give him time for a throw. He had to admit, Mason was one tough son of a bitch. At least when he wasn't hiking, that was. He grinned to himself, enjoying the banter between them. The pair had bonded almost immediately when they had first met. From their first practice session in freshman year, they could both see how well they fit together. A similar sense of humour, the same easy outgoing attitude, and their passion for the game made it easy for the pair to become fast friends. Since then, their friendship had only grown stronger both on and off the field. Neither of them were academically gifted, but that's what their girlfriends were for.

Jack grinned to himself. Both he and Mason were definitely lucky, in sport and in love.

"Dude, stop daydreaming, will you? Daylight is fading fast. We need to get back soon," Mason said, clapping a hand on Jack's shoulder and pulling him from his thoughts with a start.

"Sorry, was just thinking about the parties we'll be going to when we win the playoffs," Jack said as the pair continued walking. "There's going to be a lot of attention on me, so don't get too jealous, ok?" he added with a wide grin.

"Fuck you man, I get all the attention I need from Sarah," Mason replied with a smirk. "Anyway, you already have Christina. You can't do any better than her."

"True," Jack said absently, stopping to gaze at the vine-covered cliff they were about to reach.

Ahead of them, the fading sun cast the mountainside in a golden glow. In the dappled light, the emerald-green of the vines cascading down from the top of the mountain shimmered in the light breeze, creating a mesmerizing dance of color and shadow. The long tendrils snaked down the cliff-face in intricate patterns like nature's calligraphy, reaching the base where they dangled freely.

The pair continued walking, Jack lost in his thoughts of Christina, before Mason's words brought him back to reality once more.

"When are you going to pop the question anyway, man? Christina's a keeper and you know it," Mason said with a snigger as he pushed past.

A nervous laugh escaped Jack's lips as he shoved Mason toward the thick vines, silently hoping they'd ensnare him. He watched in astonishment as Mason stumbled, only to vanish into the creeping plants rather than becoming entangled.

A muffled "Whoa" filtered through the vine wall before they parted, revealing the excited face of Mason.

"Dude, you have to come in here. It's amazing!"

Darkness greeted Jack as he entered; the faint light from the outside was barely enough to reveal more than a few steps ahead. Waiting for his eyes to adjust, he squinted at his surroundings as they gradually became visible. They were standing in a large cave, the ceiling a good two times their height. Piles of rocks on the ground dislodged from the walls were spread throughout, the moss lining their surface an indication that they had fallen long ago. Pulling out his phone, Jack turned on its flashlight feature and swung the beam around. The cave extended at least fifty feet outward on both sides from where he stood. An earthy, damp smell filled the air. The ground beneath glistened in the light and looked slippery in areas, and the air was at least ten degrees cooler than it was outside. His phone's flashlight couldn't reach the cave's farthest end, but as he stepped forward, he saw it narrowing and extending deeper into the mountain. In the distance, the sound of dripping echoed faintly.

"This is awesome! What a find," Jack said, a smile splitting his face as he turned to high-five Mason.

Turning back to face the inky blackness ahead, he began to walk further in until he was brought to a halt by Mason's voice.

"Wait. I don't think we have time to explore right now. Don't we have to head back?"

Jack frowned, taking a quick glance down at the illuminated face of his smartwatch before sighing. Mason was right. Even if they left right now, they would be pushing it to get back to the trail before the light faded completely.

"Yeah, we do. Damn."

With today being Sunday and the week ahead being busy with the usual classes and football practice, they wouldn't be able to come back until next weekend at the earliest. Although with the team being undefeated so far this season, who knew if that was even possible if the coach decided to throw in a couple of extra training sessions to keep the momentum going. At least there was a slight chance. The game next weekend fell on a Sunday, a rarity for college football, but as this was a replay of last year's final with the top two teams, the day had been changed from Saturday to draw in more people.

"Alright, let's go then," he said, blowing out a breath in annoyance.

The pair exited the cave to the suddenly chilly, shadow-filled valley, the vanishing light of the sun lending a layer of creepiness to their surroundings.

"Hey, you know what? I just had a great idea," Jack said as he took a breath of fresh forest air.

"Cool, bro, just tell me about it on the way back to the trail. The sun is about to disappear on us," Mason said nervously, eyeing the sun now hovering just above the tree line.

With a laugh and a shake of his head, Jack led the way back toward the trail. "Dude, you have to chill out more, you're always so worried about what could go wrong that you're not seeing the opportunities right before you. Like the cave, for example," he said, clapping a hand on Mason's shoulder.

"What about the cave?" Mason asked, puzzled.

"Well, you know how Halloween is this Friday, right?" Jack asked, a smile creasing the corners of his lips as he glanced at Mason.

"Yeah, what about it?" Mason said with a confused frown.

"Bro, do I have to spell everything out for you?" Jack said with a loud laugh that sent startled birds flying from the trees as they passed underneath.

"Just tell me, man," Mason groaned. "I'm tired and hungry. You know my brain doesn't work without something in my stomach," he said, rubbing it wistfully.

"Oh, is that what it needs? Then you must be starving all the time," Jack joked, giving Mason a shove in the shoulder that sent him stumbling.

"Ha, ha, very funny," Mason said, rubbing his shoulder in a show of annoyance.

"Anyway, like I was saying, it's Halloween this Friday and now we have the perfect venue for a party," Jack finished proudly, directing a smug smile at Mason.

"You mean the cave?" Mason's eyes widened, first in surprise, then in excitement as the idea took hold.

"No, I meant the forest. Of course, I meant the cave dimwit," he said with another booming laugh that sent a fresh wave of birds skyward from the surrounding trees.

"Dude, that's like the best idea ever!" Mason exclaimed with a wide smile. "Wait, do you really think the girls would go for it, though?" His smile faded a little at the thought.

"Of course they will," Jack said, faking false bravado.

In reality, he had his doubts, but he wasn't about to voice them to Mason. Sarah would be the easiest of the two girls to convince, but Christina was another matter. Still, he would find a way. He was determined to make their last Halloween party of their college years their best one yet.

CHAPTER TWO
CHRISTINA: 27TH OCTOBER

"Mary, great job on the basket toss today. Maybe just think about what else you can do when you're up there. You still have time to spare before you descend. Julie and Sophie, make sure you practice, you're a little out of sync on the throw still," Christina called out over the clapping as the cheer squad began to disperse, the girls she mentioned giving her a nod and a wave in response.

The basket toss was a move that involved Mary being thrown up into the air by Julie and Sophie. Once up, Mary had time to perform some tricks before she descended and got caught by the two girls. All three of them were performing well, but still needed a few adjustments before they were ready to showcase it in front of a crowd.

"Alright, girls, great session today! See you same place, same time tomorrow."

Christina gave a final wave to the group before turning to make her way toward the change rooms.

"Hey you," Sarah said enthusiastically, brushing her long blonde hair back from her face as she jogged away from the group to walk alongside Christina.

"Hey," Christina said with a warm smile.

"So, are you gonna go?" Sarah asked as the pair walked through the change room door and toward the lockers and benches at the side of the room.

Christina frowned in confusion. "Go where?"

"What? You mean Jack hasn't asked you yet?"

Christina's frown deepened as she dialled her locker combination, hearing the satisfying click as it disengaged before she pulled it free. Opening the door, she pulled out her backpack and slipped it over her shoulders.

"No, he hasn't asked me anything."

Sarah laughed, shaking her head. "Typical Jack, always the last to ask."

"What is he supposed to be asking me about?" Christina said, checking her watch.

Mondays were always a rush for her, and this one even more so, considering she had a paper due tomorrow. She needed to get to the library before it closed at 5:00 pm to grab a book so she could finish her last bit of research. It was just past 4:30 pm now. Ordinarily, she wouldn't have had to rush, but because the library was being renovated, its open times were temporarily being shortened.

"Hello ladies," called out a familiar voice as the pair exited the change rooms. They turned around to see Jack and Mason jogging toward them with big smiles on their faces.

Reaching Christina, Jack enveloped her slender but athletic 5'4" body in a hug, lifting her off the ground, performing a pirouette before setting her back down again. It always surprised her how easily he did that. Sure, he was 6'1" with a body that was forged in the gym and on the sports field; even so, you'd think it would take some effort.

He gave her a quick kiss and waved at Sarah, who leapt

into Mason's arms, wrapping her legs around his body, her skirt sweeping back to reveal her toned thighs.

"Coming over to my place tonight for a 'study session?'" Jack asked, his hands miming air quotes, a playful lilt to his voice.

Christina laughed, punching him lightly in the shoulder.

"Not tonight, Romeo, I have a paper due tomorrow and I haven't finished it yet. I need to do some actual studying tonight."

"You can do some 'actual studying' at my place if you like. I'm a great helper," Jack said with a smirk and a nudge.

"You're hopeless," Christina giggled, losing herself for a moment in his confident blue eyes. "Raincheck, ok? I have to get to the library before it closes, so I'll text you later," she said, giving him a quick kiss before jogging toward the double doors leading to the courtyard outside.

"Wait, I need to..." Jack called out before the doors swung shut behind her, cutting off the rest of his sentence.

Christina sighed, checking her watch again. 4:40 pm. "Shit," she muttered under her breath as she jogged toward the library.

Christina had always been diligent in her studies. Ever since her freshman year, she had been focused and engaged, making sure she got all her work handed in on time and finishing each paper and essay well in advance. Just as well she did, too. She'd had to help Jack get his work done on top of that.

This year, though, things had been far more difficult. The increased workload, as well as juggling the pressures of leading the cheer squad and continuously assisting Jack, left her feeling constantly overwhelmed and exhausted. The thought of leaving the cheer squad, or relinquishing her captaincy, had crossed her mind, but in all honesty, she loved it. There was nothing better than seeing her squad mates grow and being involved in that growth. The girls were a tight-knit team, united by their passion and love for what they did, and the encouragement and support they offered each other was like nothing else she'd been a part of. No, she would stay on as captain this one last season. Stopping helping Jack with his work was also not on the cards. His grades needed to be kept consistently at a level that would allow him to keep his scholarship, and without her help, he was done for. Although at least Adam had been able to step in lately when she didn't have the time, which she was thankful for.

Finally reaching the library, she entered with a sigh of relief, only to hurry toward the history shelves when the librarian, Mrs. Cooke, frowned at her and pointed at the clock on the wall.

At this close to closing, the library appeared to be bare of students apart from a few who walked past her toward the exit, chatting and ignoring the library's policy for quiet, to the disapproving frown of Mrs. Cooke.

Walking through the study area, she spotted Jenny stuffing some books into her already overflowing backpack and gave her a wave when she looked up. Jenny nodded in reply, a thin, worn smile on her face, before she disappeared out of view as Christina rounded the corner to reach the shelf she needed. She scanned the row of books quickly but couldn't immediately find what she was looking for.

"Shit," she mumbled under her breath, hearing the approaching footsteps of what could only be Mrs. Cooke.

Taking a deep breath, she redoubled her efforts, finally spotting the book she needed on the bottom shelf, *The Woman's Hour: The Great Fight to Win the Vote.*

She grabbed it before Mrs. Cooke could say anything and made her way to the self-checkout scanner, adding it to her account. Casting a quick glance over her shoulder, she smiled at Mrs. Cooke, who had followed her and was standing near the exit, tapping her foot and glaring at her. Christina shoved the book into her backpack, and, with her head bowed, hurried past Mrs. Cooke, deliberately avoiding the sharp edge of her disapproving stare.

Mrs. Cooke had a reputation for being a hard ass and being unforgiving when it came to the library, its rules, and its books, and it was easy to see why. There weren't many people Christina didn't get along with, but Mrs. Cooke had always seemed to have a vendetta against her in particular. Of course, it probably didn't help that she often returned her books past their due date.

She grinned to herself as she walked out into the crisp late afternoon air, taking the opportunity to relax and clear her mind for a moment. Christina had always been a big believer in living in the present. Her mother, as alternative in her beliefs as she was, had taught her its importance, and she had often found it invaluable. She doubted she would've made it this far without that belief, given all that was on her plate.

Spotting movement out of the corner of her eye, she saw Jenny heading down the garden path between the science and math buildings toward the college gates. Despite not being in the same social circles, Christina had always held a fondness for Jenny. Although Jenny was quiet and kept mostly to herself, she was kind and non-judgemental. These were rare qualities to have in college, where everyone mostly thought about themselves and their own agendas. Jenny wasn't exactly slim but wasn't overly large either, and dressed conservatively, preferring to wear clothing one size too big. Her short brown hair, brown eyes, and glasses helped paint a picture of one who wanted to blend into the background.

Christina jogged down to join her, meeting Jenny's half-smile when she turned around upon hearing Christina's approach.

"Hey," Christina said with a warm smile.

"Hey," Jenny replied softly with a slight nod.

"So, how have you been? It's been a while since I've caught up with you."

"Yeah, I thought you'd finally given up on the pretence of trying to be friends with me." Jenny's words were laced with tension as she spoke, catching Christina off guard.

"Oh, Jenny, no, I'm sorry. It's just that things are so busy now. With this being senior year, my cheerleading, and helping my doofus boyfriend get through college, it's all a bit crazy. I've meant to catch up with you, I swear," Christina said earnestly.

Jenny glanced at her out of the corner of her eye, then dropped her head with a sigh. "Yeah, I know, I'm sorry, that was harsh. I guess things have just gotten to me lately."

"Hey, it's ok. You know I'm here for you, right? I don't want you thinking I've abandoned you."

"I don't, it's just..." Jenny hesitated, sorrow flickering across her face, the deep grooves around her eyes betraying nights spent battling restless thoughts.

"Let's go sit, yeah? And you can tell me what's going on." Christina laid her hand gently on the upper back of Jenny and guided her toward the vacant bus stop seat ahead of them as they passed through the college gates.

"So, tell me, what's been happening?" Christina asked, turning to face her and crossing her legs on the flat steel seat.

Jenny blew out a breath as a myriad of emotions passed across her face. "I caught Jeremy cheating," she said simply as tears began to well at the corners of her eyes.

"Oh, babe, I'm so sorry," Christina said, taking Jenny's hands in hers and rubbing them gently.

"His behaviour has been off for weeks now, all the typical red flags that people talk about, but I guess I just wanted to ignore them. I didn't want to believe it was happening to me, you know?" Jenny said, choking back tears.

Christina nodded, giving her space to continue.

"He would hide his phone whenever I sat next to him, constantly check it, and turn it away from me when he did. He was always smiling at the damn thing and he gave me less and less attention. He started to say he was 'too busy' to go out or meet up. I, like a fool, tried even harder to improve things between us, thinking that he was just growing bored with me." Jenny looked away, her cheeks turning a bright shade of crimson.

Christina gave her hands a squeeze, feeling her heart grow heavy with sorrow at her friend's words.

"I even had sex with him, something I swore I wasn't going to do until I was ready. Even though I wasn't, I... I didn't want to lose him, you know?"

A shuddering breath hitched in Jenny's throat as racking sobs shook her body. A torrent of tears streamed down her cheeks.

Christina uncurled her legs and scooted forward, wrapping her arms around Jenny in a comforting embrace, her heart aching for her friend.

A few minutes passed before Jenny pulled back, her face wet with tears, sniffling and wiping her eyes before she continued.

"It was afterwards, when he went to the bathroom, that his phone buzzed. I was curious to see why he was always on the damn thing, so I checked it. It was from that skank Mellissa. The message said that she 'enjoyed last night and couldn't wait to do it again tonight.' Pretty obvious what that meant, huh?"

A grimace twisted Jenny's face, halting her tears, her mouth a tight, furious line as anger flashed in her eyes.

"It turns out that asshole had been cheating on me for weeks and I had just lost my virginity to him. I dumped his sorry ass as soon as he came back from the bathroom, threw his clothes out the window, and he was forced to run outside naked to get them in broad daylight." Despite her obvious heartache, Jenny snickered, a satisfied smirk on her face.

Finding herself both shocked and amused, Christina struggled to contain her laughter at picturing Jeremy running outside naked before she could withhold it no more, and it burst out of her in a flood.

Jenny looked at her with hurt before the absurdity of the situation struck her, and she joined in. The sound of Jenny's laughter was infectious, causing Christina to laugh harder until both were doubled over, tears of mirth replacing Jenny's ones of earlier sadness.

"Oh, babe," Christina said, between giggles. "I'm so sorry that happened to you but boy, did you give that asshole what he deserved," she said, smiling in admiration as she leaned forward to give Jenny another hug.

Jenny returned her hug and leaned back, dabbing at the tears in the corners of her eyes to try to minimize the damage already done to her mascara.

"Thank you, Christina, really. I feel better for getting it off my chest. I know this is going to hurt for a while, but knowing you have my back helps a little."

"Always, babe. And please give me a call or send me a text anytime you need, ok? Day or night. I'm here for you."

Jenny nodded and gave Christina a smile before she checked her watch.

"I'd better get home. I have a test to study for. If I can concentrate on it, that is."

"Yeah, I have a paper due tomorrow myself," Christina said, sighing heavily. "Senior year is harder than I thought it would be," she admitted, feeling the stress seep back in at the thought of the work ahead.

"Well, hey, you know shooting a text goes both ways. I'm here if you want to vent," Jenny said as the pair stood up.

"Thanks, babe," Christina said.

They gave each other another brief hug before parting ways, both heading in different directions. Jenny lived on the opposite side of town, but her parents owned a cafe down Main Street just a few short blocks away, so she usually studied in the back-office area until closing time.

As Christina approached the narrow path veering off from the main one, tucked between houses across from the college, she took the opportunity to plan out the remaining work she needed to do on her paper. By the time she reached the small gate leading up the path to her house, she had a firm plan in mind.

She entered the house, popping her head through the kitchen doorway, interrupting her mom's cheerful humming as she prepared dinner to let her know she was home before trudging upstairs.

Opening the door to her room, she was greeted by its familiar orderly chaos. Books were stacked haphazardly on one side of her desk and alongside the wall closest to it, ordered by subject. Her notebooks, diary, and art book that she used to doodle in between studying for a break were in another pile on the opposite side of her desk.. Her closed laptop was positioned squarely in the middle of her desk, with her makeup and mirror behind it. To the untrained eye, it looked like any other messy college student's room, but Christina knew in an instant where everything was, and that was how she liked it.

She eyed the overflowing hamper full of dirty clothes at the end of the bed, making a mental note to do something about it before turning in. Sitting down at her desk, she placed her backpack beside her and pulled out the library book, setting it next to the laptop, which she opened and powered on.

While she waited for it to boot up, she studied herself in the mirror. She was badly in need of some TLC, but she knew it wouldn't be happening any time soon. Her naturally shiny blonde hair was still damp with perspiration from cheer squad practice after a particularly heavy session. Her normally meticulously applied makeup was patchy, a product of doing it last minute after accidentally sleeping in that morning. What most concerned her was the bags forming beneath her eyes. They had been becoming more and more noticeable over the last few weeks. She was surprised Jack hadn't brought them up. He always had his eyes on her. She cracked a smile, revealing small dimples in her cheeks. Well, he did, but his eyes weren't always on her face; they were often on her chest and legs. She wasn't exactly stacked, not like Sarah was, but he made her feel like she was all the same, and she wasn't mad about it.

Her phone vibrating in her pocket brought her back to reality, but she ignored it. She needed to get her work done first. Refocusing on her laptop, she opened up her essay, sat back, and released a sigh. There were times when she regretted choosing to study subjects that would take her to law school, and this was one of them. The subject matter could be so damn depressing. She stared at the essay, the title, "Shattering the Chains: The Struggle and Triumph of the Women's Suffrage Movement," sitting at the forefront of the screen before her. Taking a deep breath, she started typing.

By the time she'd finished with only a quick break to eat dinner, it was 10:00 pm. She could barely keep her eyes open when she finally sent off her work on the student portal and closed the laptop, and she still needed to take a shower. She did so, quickly. Her bed was calling to her, and all she wanted to do was to collapse into it. Her eyes fell on the hamper of dirty clothes, remembering they badly needed tending to. They could wait; another day wouldn't hurt.

After getting into her pyjamas, brushing her teeth, and slipping between the sheets of her bed, she plugged in her phone and set it down on her nightstand beside her when it flashed with a notification. Recalling the phone vibration in her pocket when she sat down to do her work earlier that night, she hesitated. She was torn between checking her messages and just saying to hell with it and switching off the light to sleep. Another notification flashing on the phone made the decision for her.

Picking it up, she tapped on the message. It was from Jack. Of course it was. She loved the guy, but he could be so clingy sometimes, especially when he wanted something.

5:20 pm Babe, you there?

5:33 pm I need to ask you something.
Text me back when you can

6:43 pm I'm just gonna go ahead and
assume you've lost yourself in study.

6:44 pm You're never gonna guess what me and Mason found on our hike yesterday.

6:45 pm It was a cave! Pretty sure it had never been found before either.

6:46 pm Now you might be asking yourself why I'm bringing this up.

6:46 pm Simple

6:48 pm It's Halloween Friday night. How about you, me, Mason, and Sarah have ourselves a night to remember?

6:50 pm I'm talking cave party baby! I know right? You must be thinking about how lucky you are to have such an amazing boyfriend like me right now.

6:52 pm You can thank me later if you know what I mean 😜

10:11 pm Hey you, hope you're not studying too hard. Just wanted to say I love you. I'll see you tomorrow and you can let me know how amazing I am then 🩶

Christina scrolled through the messages, shaking her head at first in shock, then in amusement. Being Jack's girlfriend was nothing if not interesting. Sometimes she didn't understand where his head was at, but she couldn't help but love the fool.

She let out a little chuckle and put the phone back on

her nightstand face down. If she responded now, she would no doubt be up for hours chatting with him.

She lay back and closed her eyes, drifting off almost immediately into a deep, dreamless sleep.

Chapter Three
Jenny: 28th October

Shouldering her backpack, Jenny exited the study hall. Shuffling to the side of the door, she leaned against the wall and closed her eyes. Now that her classes and her tutoring lessons were over for the day, she had to return to the pain of reality.

It had been a few days now since she had ended things with Jeremy. Though she had expected to feel down, she had thought that maybe, inexplicably, she would start feeling better by now. She now knew that was wishful thinking. Being with Jeremy for the last few years had become a comfort, an escape that she had used to get away from the difficulties of the real world. A lifetime of harsh self-judgment and pessimism had been her norm until Jeremy entered her life, bringing with him a much-needed balance. Now she found herself questioning things. Had she done the right thing by dumping him? What if she had just thrown away the one chance at love she'd ever have?

She sighed, her thoughts drifting to ways of apologizing to Jeremy and begging him for a second chance before she caught herself. No. He had deserved what he got. She had to have more respect for herself. She needed to be strong and take the time to find herself again. It was one thing to tell herself that, but entirely another story to do it. Tears formed at the corners of her eyes, and she wiped them away angrily. Pushing herself off the wall, she began to walk toward the exit.

"Hey you," a soft voice called out from behind her.

She turned to see the smiling but sweat-lined face of Christina, who had just come through the gymnasium exit, the doors swinging closed behind her.

"Hey, yourself," Jenny said, managing a small, tired smile.

Christina's smile faltered, replaced by a worried frown.

"Are you ok?"

"Not really," Jenny admitted, blinking back the tears that threatened to spill. "It's just that things are harder than I thought. Apparently, break-ups are hard, who knew?" she said, forcing a laugh.

Christina nodded sympathetically, approaching her and giving her a hug.

"Boys suck. I swear I'm never getting into a relationship again," Jenny said as they parted.

The pair resumed walking, Jenny leading the way toward the exit..

"You can have Jack if you want. He's driving me crazy at the moment," Christina said, laughing and shaking her head.

"Um... No thanks, he's not really my type," Jenny said, with a small chuckle of her own. "What's he doing now?"

"Well, for starters, trying to juggle being his constant tutor and his girlfriend is tough and always will be. Luckily, Adam is helping out a bit more on that side these days. But now he's come up with a ridiculous idea for Halloween."

Despite herself, Jenny began to feel her sadness ebb

away. Christina always had a calming presence and was easy to talk to. She had never thought that Christina, one of the prettiest and most popular girls in school and the cheer squad captain, would even notice her, let alone talk to her. But Christina broke the mould of what she had expected. Movies and TV always portrayed her type as being stuck up and arrogant, but this was about as far from the truth as it can get when it came to Christina.

"Oh really? Surely it can't be that bad." Jenny couldn't help but giggle at the strained expression of pain on Christina's face.

"Oh, it's bad alright," Christina said with a sigh as the two reached the double doors of the exit. Jenny pushed through and held a door open for Christina as she passed, letting it swing shut behind her.

"So, you know how Halloween is this Friday, right?"

Jenny nodded, eyeing Christina with curiosity.

"God, I can't believe it's even something I have to mention," she muttered, shaking her head in disdain.

"Jack and Mason went hiking on Sunday and found a cave and now Jack wants to host a Halloween party there with Mason and Sarah and I don't want to go, and it sounds like the worst idea ever and I'm sure it will be cold and smelly because of bats and stuff," she said in a rush, her face turning a bright sheen of red.

Jenny stood there open-mouthed, before she burst out in a peal of laughter.

"Oh my god, you poor thing," she said after a few moments. "That sounds horrifying and not in the scary, spooky way," she laughed again, all her pain temporarily forgotten.

"It is. It's going to be," Christina said miserably.

"Well, hey, at least it will be different. Something to tell your future children about."

"Oh god, don't mention children. Not until I'm old, like thirty or something."

"Thirty isn't old," Jenny laughed.

"Yeah. I know, you're right. It just seems old when you're twenty-one," Christina said, a small smile on her lips.

"So, what are you going to do? Are you going to go?"

Christina sighed, her shoulders slumping in resignation. "I guess I have to. I mean, Jack is so excited about it. He's adamant that he wants this Halloween to be special. You know, because it's our last one as seniors and all."

Jenny nodded, still amused by Christina's situation as they strolled along the afternoon sun-drenched garden path toward the college gates.

"Well, hey, I've gotta get back home, but message me if you want to vent more, ok? Don't suffer in silence." Jenny laughed once more.

Christina gave her a hug, and the pair parted. As Jenny exited the college, she turned to head towards University Avenue, which would take her the rest of the way to Marshall Square Mall.

It wasn't until she entered the bustling mall and saw the familiar sign of "Orange Bean Cafe" that she realised she hadn't thought of Jeremy at all since before Christina came and talked to her. She inserted her earbuds and scrolled through her playlists on her phone, settling on "Jenny's Ultimate Energy Mix." Waving to her mom, who was at the registers serving a customer, she walked through the open door and through the swing gate beside the counter display on her way into the office. Perhaps there was hope and a way through the pain after all.

Chapter Four
Christina

Ding!

Christina's phone on the desk popped up yet another message notification, and she groaned in annoyance.

"Aren't you gonna answer that?" Luna asked, swinging around to face Christina, her wide brown eyes filled with curiosity. Christina, with a hairbrush in one hand, glanced at her and gave her a brief smile before glaring at her phone in frustration.

"Later. It can wait. It's just my friends being annoying."

"What are they annoying you about?" Luna asked.

"Just some stupid party they want me to go to," Christina said, swivelling the chair Luna was seated in back to face the mirror to resume brushing Luna's lush black hair.

"Oh, a party! That sounds fun. Can I come?"

Luna's hopeful expression made Christina smile. At thirteen years old, Luna was full of the innocence of youth and still held the carefree attitude to reflect it. If Christina had the power, she would freeze time for Luna right now so she could remain like that before the complexities of growing up began to eat her childhood away. It didn't help that Luna was starting to lose her baby fat. Her future beauty was beginning to shine through, and it made Christina want to protect her all the more.

"It's going to be in a cave. It will be cold, smelly, and dark, and there will probably be loads of bats, so somehow, I don't think you'd want to," she said with a sigh.

"Ewwwww, no thanks," Luna said, scrunching up her face in disgust.

"Exactly what I think, too," Christina said with a laugh as she ran the brush through Luna's hair one last time before setting it down on the desk.

"There you go," Christina said with a smile filled with adoration, placing her hands on Luna's shoulders and watching her as she studied herself in the mirror.

Luna turned her head from side to side, checking her hair to ensure it was tangle-free.

"Thanks, sis," she said brightly.

Christina's phone dinged and lit up with another message. The bright glow of the screen felt almost like an accusation, an insistent cry for her attention.

Taking a deep breath and then blowing it out slowly, Christina scooped up the phone, gave Luna a kiss on her forehead, and retreated to her room next door. Lying on her bed, she scrolled through the notifications.

Ever since Jack had cornered her in the cafeteria earlier at lunchtime and told her about his plans for Halloween, he had been badgering her about coming. It felt like it was all he had talked about all day. To make matters worse, he had gotten Sarah and Mason involved, too. The trio had formed a group chat, and ever since then, her phone had been blowing up with messages, making it almost impossible to concentrate on studying. Sure, she could have muted the notifications, but she'd always had a compulsion to people please, and it felt like if she didn't respond every now and again, the others would take offense. They wouldn't, of course, she knew that, but it still felt wrong to ignore them. She had to give them an answer at some point, but she really, really didn't want to go.

Closing her eyes, she tried to think of excuses. She could say that her parents wanted to go away this weekend to visit relatives, and she was being dragged along with them. No, it was too suspiciously last-minute. She could say Luna was sick and she had to take care of her. That wouldn't work either. They would just say her parents could look after her. She couldn't even say she'd gotten injured at cheer squad practice or had to study because Sarah was both in the cheer squad and her classes and would know she was lying.

No, she would have to go. Just then, a thought popped into her head. What if she invited Jenny? If she said she would only go if Jenny came too, then it would kill two birds with one stone. She could share in the pain with someone else, and it would serve to distract Jenny and get her out of the house. Who knows, perhaps they could somehow even end up having some fun.

She grinned to herself. A small part of her felt bad that she was about to drag Jenny into this predicament with her, but a bigger part felt growing excitement at the prospect. Plus, she knew Jenny was a good sport and hoped she would go along with it. It would be good for her to be social rather than mope about Jeremy, who wasn't worth it.

She opened the chat and began to type.

Mason 5:44 pm: Who's Jenry?

Sarah 5:46 pm: Jenny really? She's gonna bring the whole mood down

Mason 5:47 pm: I agree, tho I still don't know who she is.

Sarah 5:48 pm: Yes you do, you're in classes with her.

Mason 5:49 pm: Nope, the name doesn't ring a bell.

Sarah 5:50 pm: She's the quiet super smart one that sits at the back. The one with glasses and short brown hair. The one that Adam is crazy for.

Mason 5:52 pm: Still no idea.

Sarah 5:55 pm: *sigh* I give up

Jack 6:02 pm: Well if it will get you to come then I'm ok with it. Ok with everyone else?

Sarah 6:06 pm: Fine I guess.

Mason 6:12 pm: Sure, the more the merrier.

Jack 6:20 pm: You know what? I just had another brilliant idea.

Christina 6:23 pm: *groan*

Jack 6:25 pm: You can thank Mason for this one.

Mason 6:27 pm: Who me? What did I do?

Jack 6:33 pm: If Jenny is coming, then I think we invite Adam too. Might spark some fireworks.

Christina 6:34 pm: NO. THAT'S THE LAST THING SHE NEEDS. SHE JUST BROKE UP WITH JEREMY!

Mason 6:37 pm: Well I think it's a great idea.

Sarah 6:38 pm: I'm with Christina on this one.

Mason 6:39 pm: Of course you are, you're always on her side.

Sarah 6:41 pm: Be thankful that I am. I would have dumped your ass by now otherwise.

Mason 6:42 pm: Thanks Christina!

Jack 6:44 pm: Fine, alright then Adam is out. Jenny is in if she wants to come.

Christina 6:50 pm: I'll invite her tomorrow. Until then, stop spamming me with messages. I've got studying to do.

Mason 6:52 pm: Ok Ms bookworm

Christina set down her phone with a smile. Sometimes her friends drove her crazy, but she wouldn't change them for the world. Despite their differences, their friendship somehow just worked.

Chapter Five
Jenny: 29th October

Jenny absentmindedly turned the page of her book, occasionally looking up to see if anyone was watching her, a habit she had developed without even realizing it. At this point, the action was ingrained, as automatic as breathing. It all started in elementary school. As a skinny, nerdy girl who liked to keep to herself, she had been a prime target for bullies. She had often used the library as a refuge, but all too often she was followed there. Grabbing a book, she would settle at a table and endure the stares, giggles, and mocking faces directed at her until the troublemakers were eventually caught by a librarian and told to leave. She had grown so used to being stared at that looking up from her book every now and again to survey her surroundings had become a tic. Often an annoying one that interrupted her flow when she was lost in her book.

She really should see someone about it. Those days were long gone, and it was a habit she didn't need anymore.

"Hey you," Christina's voice floated from behind her, breaking her out of her reverie.

"Oh, hey," Jenny said with a smile. Christina rounded

the table, setting her backpack on the floor, and collapsed into the seat next to her.

"You look like how I feel," Jenny said, noticing the heavy bags under Christina's eyes, a reflection of her own exhaustion.

"Gee, thanks," Christina laughed softly, conscious of the people around studying, some of whom still gave her an annoyed stare.

Jenny put her book face down on the table and studied Christina, who was now scowling at her phone. Something felt off about Christina today—an unusual tension in the way she was carrying herself. For as long as she'd known her, since freshman year, she hadn't seen her even half as stressed as Christina appeared now. A product, she guessed, born from Christina's mom's calming influence and teachings of mindfulness.

"Everything ok?" Jenny asked, her forehead creasing in concern.

With a sigh, Christina looked up from her phone, placing it face down on the table. Leaning back in her chair, the lines of exhaustion were clearly visible on her weary face.

"Yeah, it's just been a hard and frustrating week, you know?"

Jenny nodded in sympathy, giving Christina space to continue.

With a slow, drawn-out exhalation, Christina leaned forward again.

"OK, so I'm just going to come out and ask," she blurted out, a pained expression written on her face.

Jenny nodded, encouraging her to continue, curious as to where this was going to go.

"You know that Halloween party I was complaining to you about? The one in the cave?"

Jenny nodded once more.

Christina looked down, fidgeting nervously with her phone case. "Well, Jack, Mason, and Sarah have been bugging me about it constantly. And um... well... I may have said that I'd only go if you came," she looked away, her face turning red.

Jenny blinked a couple of times, trying to process what Christina had said.

"You... want me to come?"

Christina looked in her direction but avoided meeting her gaze.

"I'm sorry, I know I shouldn't have said it but I was trying to come up with some excuse and last night the idea to invite you came into my mind and it felt like a good idea at the time but now I think it's just stupid and I shouldn't have brought it up."

If Christina's face was red before, it was positively shining like a beacon now.

"Wow," Jenny said, the words finally starting to sink in. "Wow," she repeated. "Well, I guess it could be fun," she said slowly.

"Wait... what?" Christina's loud, relieved voice cut through the quiet murmur of the neighbouring tables, prompting further frowns from those seated there.

"You're going to come?" she asked in a strained whisper.

"Yeah... Yeah, let's do it," Jenny said, beginning to warm to the idea. "I mean, I just feel so horrible all the time. I'm angry, I'm sad, I'm scared, I'm disappointed. I'm all of those things, and Jeremy shouldn't get to make me feel that way. He's not worth it. Maybe this is a way to forget about things. For a little while at least."

"You don't mind that it's going to be just us? I don't want to make you feel uncomfortable, you know, with us being couples and everything," Christina said, smiling uncertainly at Jenny.

"It's ok, really. I can handle it. I mean, the boys will probably be too busy giving each other shit to worry about us girls anyway, am I right?"

Christina's laughter rang out, and she nodded, clapping a hand over her mouth to try to muffle the sound. The glare of the approaching Mrs. Cooke suggested her attempt had ended in failure.

"Oh shit," Christina muttered, noticing her approach. "Well, um, I'll catch you later, ok? I'll text you about the plans when I find them out." She shouldered her backpack and walked towards the exit, keeping her head down to avoid the glare of Mrs. Cooke, who had stopped halfway to their table and was standing stiffly with hands on hips.

Jenny giggled before catching herself. Mrs. Cooke glanced at her with disapproval before she retreated towards the front desk.

Jenny looked down at the book lying face down on the table and thought about picking it up again and continuing where she left off, but her interest was gone.

She sighed, picked it up, and walked over to the returns trolley to place it back where she had found it. Reading had always been an escape for her, but it just wasn't working this time. Perhaps this cave party, as bizarre as it sounded, was just what she needed.

Chapter Six
Adam

Adam studied the field from the bleachers, watching Jack and Mason make their last play of their practice match. He'd often pictured himself there alongside them, another hero of the team, but it wasn't to be. Year after year, he crashed and burned during tryouts, relegated to cheering from the sidelines. This particular practice match was different in that the coach had chosen to test Mason's defensive skills by placing him in the middle linebacker position, essentially making him the quarterback of the defence. Leaning forward in his seat, he watched with interest as the play began.

Dropping back from the scrimmage, Jack scanned the field, searching for an opening as bodies clashed together and grunts of effort filled the air. Mason, his sights set on Jack, charged forward, ready to break through the offensive line.

Jack spotted an opening and took the small window of opportunity offered. With a flick of his wrist, he sent the ball spiralling through the air toward the intended receiver. Mason, knowing Jack's game inside and out, was one step ahead. Anticipating the pass, he leapt into the air with impressive agility, the trait he was most well-known for on the team. Despite his well-timed jump, his fingers only just managed to graze the ball. Still, it was enough to disrupt the trajectory, and it spilled to the ground. The whistle was blown, ending the game and leaving Mason's side the winner.

Erupting in cheers, the team gathered around Mason, slapping him on the back and helmet enough to send him collapsing to the ground laughing. Jack jogged up to him, his own helmet tucked under his arm, and offered his hand to him with a smile on his face.

Standing up from the bleachers, Adam made his way down to the field to congratulate his two friends for the brilliant sequence of play.

"Dude, you've been on fire today. Keep that up, and we might just win this weekend," Jack was saying as Adam approached from behind the pair.

"That's the aim, my man," Mason said with a grin as he took the offered hand and hauled himself to his feet. "We better make sure we don't get too shitfaced this Friday though," Mason added as he removed his helmet and wiped a sheen of sweat from his brow with his elbow.

"Going to be hard not to, given we now have Jenny coming," Jack said with an eye roll.

"She's probably gonna be a downer the whole night."

"What are you guys talking about?" Adam said, trying to interject himself into the conversation.

"Oh... er... nothing," Mason said, exchanging a quick glance with Jack.

"Wait a minute," Jack said thoughtfully, a smile dawning on his face. He whirled to face Mason, leaving Adam bewildered and feeling like an outsider to their odd exchange.

"I know what I said on the chat, but I really think Adam here could be the solution to our problem."

"Hey... yeah... you're right!" Mason said, clearly confused but still eager to follow Jack's lead. "Um... Just one thing. What problem?" Mason said, a sheepish expression forming on his face.

"Oh man. Seriously," Jack said, feigning a slap to his forehead. "The party? Our Jenny problem?"

"Oh right... Wait... on the chat, you said-" Mason began before Jack cut him off.

"I know what I said, man, but do you really wanna put up with a downer all night?" Jack said. By the look on Mason's face, he knew he had said enough to convince him.

"Hey guys, I'm right here, you know. What Jenny problem? Can someone tell me what's going on?" Adam said, his voice tight with barely suppressed frustration.

"OK, here's the deal," Jack began, turning back to face him. "I found this really cool cave when Mason and I were hiking together, and with Halloween coming up Friday, I thought it would be a great place to host a Halloween party. At first, we thought to keep it small, you know? I mean, I didn't want people to discover the cave and ruin it for everyone by getting the party shut down, so it was only going to be just us and the girls." Jack paused for a moment when he noticed Adam's expression.

Jack's words stirred up a maelstrom of feelings in Adam. His initial agitation morphed into jealousy, then an aching sadness, as the cold, hard truth of his exclusion sank in. After everything he'd done for them over the last few years, it was a bitter pill to swallow. He had helped both of them with their homework, letting them borrow his notes, and even lending some of his work to copy and occasionally completing assignments for them. After all that, he'd thought it would be enough to break him into the friendship group that seemed to perpetually be just Mason and Jack.

The pull of popularity had always been a siren song for him, despite his knowing it was foolish to chase it. He was too quiet for the jocks, too loud for the bookworms; a lonely figure navigating the college social scene with no real place to call home. He had an ordinary appearance; not ugly or handsome, just average, a face that didn't stand out. His almond eyes, his military style haircut, shaved at the sides and longer at the top, couldn't disguise the early indications of a receding hairline. Despite going to the gym regularly, he could never get himself toned the way he wanted to be. In almost every way except academically, he was just another average guy most people ignored. Only with fewer friends. His people-pleasing tendency hadn't helped with that. He knew he came across as a little too desperate to others, which was probably the reason why he hadn't made any real, genuine friends. He couldn't help it, though. From what he had learned in psychology, he knew that his behaviour stemmed back to the way he was raised, but he didn't want to explore that particular avenue. That path, as necessary as it would eventually be, was fraught with the thorns of self-discovery, promising pain and suffering, and his life was already difficult enough.

Adam forced himself to focus back on the conversation, nodding with a carefully neutral face that couldn't quite mask the wounded look in his eyes.

Jack glanced at Mason nervously before continuing, "So, um, anyway, Christina didn't want to come, and eventually, she said she'd only come if she could invite Jenny." He smiled anxiously at Adam. "So, ah, we know how you kind of like, have a thing for Jenny, and you know, now that she's available, we thought that maybe you'd like to come too."

Adam could feel himself shrinking inside. It was as if the life he'd foolishly constructed, a fragile illusion, had suddenly and violently collided with reality, staining the edges of his carefully curated world. He knew now, without a doubt, that he was just being used by the two of them. Stupid thing is, he had known it all along but just hadn't wanted to admit it, content to just pretend like he was part of the crew. He plastered a smile on his face, his eyes conveying his true feelings, which Jack and Mason either failed to notice or ignored.

"Well, putting it that way, how can I resist coming?" Adam said, forcing a laugh.

Relief washed over Jack's face, the stiffness in his posture melting away as he grinned at Adam and gave him a hearty clap on his back.

"Awesome man, we would love to have you there."

Jack took a step back and placed his hands on Adam's shoulders, looking him in the eyes.

"Hey man, you know we would have invited you if we were gonna invite anyone else. We'd just planned it as a couple's thing, you know?" He grinned at Adam, releasing his grip and slapping him on the back again. "And who knows, it might just end up a couples thing anyway by the end of the night, hey?" He gave Adam a playful nudge.

Despite the heavy weight in his chest, a small smile touched Adam's lips as he considered the possibility. This might be fun after all, he thought to himself, feeling his spirits begin to lift the more he thought about the party ahead.

CHAPTER SEVEN
CHRISTINA: 31ST OCTOBER

"Come on, man, hurry up, will you?" Jack yelled, watching Adam's slow progress behind him in the distance as he struggled to catch up.

"Hey, I would be a lot faster if you guys helped carry some of this crap for me," Adam hollered back, hefting one of the two twenty-four cases of Bud Light into the air and shaking it.

"Hey, that's precious cargo. Be careful with that," Jack yelled, shaking his head, a mischievous glint in his eyes.

"Be nice to him, Jack, you did ask him to carry a lot, you know," Christina said beside him. A faint smile hovered on her lips as she watched the scene unfold.

"Yeah? Well, if HE had found this cave, maybe I would be helping." He directed his gaze towards Mason, wearing a devilish grin. "Speaking of which, YOU should be down there helping him, too."

"Screw you man. I found that cave first," Mason said, giving him a playful shove to his shoulder.

"Yeah, in your dreams maybe," Jack said with an obnoxiously loud laugh.

"Cut it out, you two," Sarah groaned from behind them, her voice dripping with mock exasperation. "I'm getting tired just listening to you both, and the night hasn't even begun," she said in a playful tone. She squeezed between Mason and Jack, her breasts lightly brushing against both of their arms as she made her way up the scree-covered slope.

"Hey babe, wait up," Mason said, his eyes drifting to her ass as he trotted after her and draped an arm over her shoulder, pulling her close.

Christina couldn't help but groan at the antics of her friend. Sarah was an intentional tease and flirt, but it had always been harmless. Sarah's eyes were set firmly on Mason. Christina could see what was going to happen tonight a mile away, though. Sarah was dressed in a short skirt that barely covered her ass and an equally short tight tank top which wouldn't exactly keep her warm in the no doubt cold and dank cave. Christina would have to brace herself for some PDA between the two. Shaking off that depressing thought, she redirected her focus to Jenny.

"You ok, Jenny?" Christina said, her brow furrowing with concern as she looked behind them at the slowly approaching girl.

"Yeah, just tired is all," Jenny said with a nonchalant shrug, avoiding Christina's gaze.

Christina inwardly sighed, feeling a heavy weight settle in her chest. She had hoped that inviting her to the party tonight would lift Jenny's spirits or at least provide a temporary escape from her heartache. Initially, it seemed to have worked, but ever since then, she had seen her cautious excitement fade away as the time for the party approached. Once the group had arrived and started their journey up the mountain, she seemed distant and down-hearted. Perhaps it was because of the way the two couples reminded her of what she'd lost. Or maybe it was because of Adam. She had been furious at first when she found out Jack had gone ahead and invited him despite her telling him not to. He'd explained that Adam had overheard himself and Mason talking about the party after football practice, and he felt guilty, so he felt like he had to. She had to wonder if that was really the truth; it seemed awfully convenient. She just hoped Adam didn't ruin Jenny's night with his presence. Everyone knew that he had a thing for her. Christina had to laugh at that. He had no chance.

"Come on," she said, as she encircled her arm around Jenny's and gave it a gentle, comforting rub. "I promise, tonight will be a night to remember. We have music, great company, alcohol, and don't forget these," she said, a mischievous smile on her face as she pulled out a pack of joints and wiggled them in front of Jenny.

Jenny glanced at them, a subtle smile forming on her lips, and she released a soft chuckle. "I'm not sure I'll remember tonight by the sounds of all that." Jenny's eyes fixed on the approaching cliff face, her jaw tightening with resolute determination. "But maybe that's what I need, just to forget everything for a while."

"Exactly," Christina responded, giving her a gentle nudge and a comforting smile. "Hey, maybe Adam can help with that too," she said, winking at her and giving her a few more suggestive nudges.

"Adam?" Jenny's brow furrowed, a flicker of confusion showing in her eyes.

"What, you didn't know? He's into you, girl," Christina said with a giggle.

"What? Really? Him?" Jenny's gaze shifted to Adam, who was lagging behind. Their eyes connected, and a radiant, goofy-looking smile illuminated his face.

Giggling, the pair quickened their pace to catch up with the three ahead of them.

The sparse tree covering on the slope allowed the late afternoon sun to filter through, casting long shadows on the uneven surface they walked upon. The air here felt invigoratingly fresh, a stark contrast to the overpowering scent of weed, perfume, aftershave, and sweaty clothes that permeated the hormone-charged dorms where they had met the boys before departing. Above them, the sky was a breathtaking shade of fading blue, streaked with pink and orange from the setting sun, interrupted only by the occasional passing flock of birds. Meanwhile, the rustling of leaves and distant sounds of wildlife searching for food added a lively energy to their peaceful surroundings.

With a deep breath, Christina felt the tension melting away from her body. Her senses came alive as excitement started to surge through her. Halloween was her favourite time of the year, and the prospect of the upcoming party in the cave had grown on her despite her initial resistance to the idea.

Upon reaching a clearing, the girls heard the boys ahead whooping, their voices bouncing off the expansive, treeless, and stony slope that lay ahead.

"Sounds like the party has already started," Christina said, shaking her head with a smile of amusement. "Are you ready for this?" she asked Jenny, her voice gentle and warm, her eyes filled with concern. "If you're not, just say the word. We can leave right now if you want to. It might be your last chance before it gets too dark, though." She indicated the fading sun, which was now barely visible above the cliff face in front of them.

"No, it's ok. I'm ready," Jenny said, her voice filled with a nervous hitch.

With some difficulty, the two girls scrambled up the

steep hill the slope had turned into, their feet slipping a few times on the loose shale, until they reached a small plateau. A wall of rock, almost vertical, stretched out before them. Moss and sinuous vines decorated it, their bright green hues shimmering in the waning orange light of the sunset.

"Would you look at that." Christina murmured, her voice barely audible as she turned slowly, savoring every angle of the magnificent sight. From this vantage point, they could see the peaks and valleys of the mountains surrounding them, and the rustling trees below, their leaves a tapestry of autumn hues.

"It's beautiful," said Jenny, mirroring Christina in her movements.

Startled by crackling behind the draping green vines at the cliff face behind them, they spun around. Pushing aside the plants, Jack greeted them with a proud smile and eyes filled with excitement.

"Welcome to my humble abode," he said, sweeping his arm out to present the cave with a graceful bow.

"You mean our abode," Mason shouted, his voice booming from somewhere within.

"Yeah, yeah," Jack said with a grin, holding the vines aside to let the approaching girls enter.

"Wow, this is amazing!" Christina said, ducking her head under one of the vine's roots protruding from the top of the cave's entrance. Jack acknowledged Jenny with a nod as she walked past, and he allowed the vines to fall behind them. Both girls dumped their backpacks and sleeping bags on the floor next to the others before taking a look around.

The boys had already set up lanterns at points along both sides of the cave walls. Each one was Halloween-themed, their creepy grins casting eerie shadows on the walls. A few stray golden rays of sunlight filtered through the tangled vines, illuminating the jagged archway of the cave entrance.

"Um... are you guys sure this cave is safe?" Jenny asked with furrowed brows, her voice filled with worry. She pointed to the cracks lining the surface above the archway. The thin fractures seemed poised to widen and cause a collapse with even the slightest disturbance.

"Relax, it'll be fine," Jack said with a laugh, his voice echoing through the cave, attempting to alleviate the tension of Jenny's question. The girls exchanged unsure glances, their eyes darting back and forth between the boys.

"Do you see any rocks on the floor? If it was that unstable, there would be some signs of them coming loose recently," Mason said, backing Jack up.

"Exactly," Jack chimed in cheerfully, emphasizing the point. "Now, how about we get this party started?" he said with a roguish grin, pulling Christina toward him and giving her a long, lingering kiss.

"Whoa, get a room, why don't ya," Mason said in an overly loud voice, eliciting giggles from Sarah, who was sitting next to him.

"Hey, did I miss something?" said the puffing figure of Adam as he pushed through the vines, struggling and entangling himself in them to the laughter of everyone else in the cave.

"Glad you guys are having fun," he muttered with a hint of sarcasm, placing the beer cases on the ground and dumping his backpack and sleeping bag so he could free himself from the entangling vines.

After a few more laughs at Adam's expense, the group got to work setting up the cave.

Chapter Eight
Adam

After disentangling himself from the vines, Adam collected his backpack and sleeping bag and dumped them next to the others. He then dragged over the beer cases and joined the group who were piling rocks to create a makeshift fire pit. Once done, Mason and Sarah offered to search for wood outside the cave for the fire, while Jack and Christina volunteered to arrange the battery-operated string lights on the cave walls. Jenny and Adam had the task of finishing the decorating, strategically placing various props and small Halloween-themed battery-operated animatronic creatures throughout the cave.

"So, ah, how are you doing? Everything ok?" Adam said with a wince, the forced casualness of his tone betraying his nervousness, an uncomfortable tension hanging in the air between them.

"I'm not so great, but I'll be ok," Jenny replied, a small smile forming at the corner of her mouth, appreciating the effort but eager to change topics. "So, what made you decide to become the pack rat for this expedition into the unknown?" she said, her voice tinged with a hint of playfulness.

Adam felt his heart quicken. Was she flirting with him? The cave was dimly lit, obscuring her face, so he couldn't tell if she was smiling or not.

"Umm... well, I'm a real Halloween fanatic, so naturally, when I heard the guys talking about their plans for a cave party and Jack asked me if I wanted to come, I said yes. It beats taking my little brother out trick or treating this year, that's for sure." The words escaped his lips, accompanied by a jittery laugh, the volume much higher than he had expected.

"Oh, your poor brother, he's going to be so disappointed," Jenny said, her tone losing its playful quality.

"Oh no, he'll be fine. He got invited to go out with his friends, he doesn't need big brother anymore," he said, his words tumbling out in a rush when he caught the shift in her voice.

Minutes passed in awkward silence before Adam spoke again.

"I, uh, I sort of wanted to come too when I found out you were coming," he said, his voice trembling nervously.

"Oh... Ummm, I'm sorry, Adam," Jenny stammered awkwardly. "I'm not really interested in seeing anyone right now. It's just... with my breakup being so recent and all..." Her words hung in the air, but her body language spoke volumes as she subtly edged away from him.

"Oh, it's..."

"Hey guys, take a look at this," Jack interrupted from the back of the cave, his voice brimming with excitement.

Eager to avoid the awkward conversation, Jenny set down the prop she was holding and made a beeline toward Jack. With a soft, exasperated sigh, Adam smacked his forehead, berating himself. This wasn't what he had planned to do or say at all. Now he'd ruined any chance he had with Jenny. Or thought he may have had at any rate. Maybe there had been no chance at all, he thought to himself, reflecting on what she'd said. With another sigh escaping his lips, he reluctantly followed Jenny, his heart heavy in his chest.

Chapter Nine
Christina

Christina finished setting up the last of her string lights and followed the distant flashlight glow of Jack, hearing the footsteps of Jenny and Adam following behind.

She could see Jack peering at something at the end of the cave as she approached. He turned to face her, his gestures full of enthusiasm as he pointed towards an opening in the cave walls.

Even as far back as she was, Christina could smell the dank air wafting toward her from its depths. As she neared him, she could make out the size of the gap—just wide enough to fit through, but it would be a tight squeeze. Anyone who tried would likely have their clothes torn to shreds, judging by the jagged edges of some of the rocks on either side.

"What's so exciting? It's just a hole," Christina said, unimpressed, stopping next to Jack and looking at him with an eyebrow raised.

"It's not the hole," he said with a smirk. "It's what's inside it. Here, take a look." Stepping aside, he directed the beam of the flashlight through the gap.

Christina moved closer, squinting her eyes as they followed the glaring light. At first, all she could see besides the walls was a pitch-black void beyond the gap, indicating another cavernous space. Confused, she was just about to ask what she was supposed to be seeing when a dark shape darted across the beam of the flashlight. She gasped in surprise. Its two glowing eyes seemed to stare directly at her before disappearing in an instant. In the brief glimpse she caught of it, the thing was roughly bat-shaped but appeared oddly malformed.

"Wha... What the heck is that? That doesn't look like any bat I've ever seen."

"I know, right? How cool is it? There's a few of them in there. I saw more fly past while I was waiting. We have our very own live Halloween creepy creatures."

The cave filled with the sound of his booming laughter, which seemed to carry and intensify through the gap as it reached the other side, making the creatures stir further in agitation.

Angry screeches reverberated from the other side of the gap, starting with just a few, then growing in intensity as more joined in, creating a chaotic symphony that only seemed to rile up the creatures even more. The sound of rapidly approaching wings began to fill the air, wiping the smile off Jack's face and causing an icy chill of fear to shoot down Christina's spine. He nervously shifted his gaze between her and the gap. With the beam from the flashlight still trained on the opening, he reached for her hand and gripped it as they slowly retreated.

CHAPTER TEN
ADAM

"Hey guys, what's going on? What's that sound?" Adam asked, his voice laced with curiosity as he neared Jack and Christina. He was a few steps ahead of Jenny, who trailed close behind.

"I think I just made some ugly ass bats angry," Jack said, glancing back at Adam with a forced grin.

"Wha…" Adam started to respond, but his words were cut short as a swarm of small, dark-winged creatures burst out from the gap, hurtling straight towards them.

"Oh shit!" Jack shouted in panic and began running, pulling Christina along with him.

Adam froze in shock, unable to react quickly enough to follow before the swarm flew at and by him, leaving behind a noxious odor of guano, urine, and a sour scent that almost made him vomit.

Jenny reacted quicker than Adam and had just turned tail to run when the bats came toward her. A dozen of the animals, larger than the smaller forms that flew past, veered off from the pack to head for her, their elongated talons tangling in her clothes as they screeched and batted their wings against her body. The sound of her piercing scream filled the air as the talons tore through her clothes, seeking the tender flesh underneath. Her arms flailed frantically, attempting to swat away the relentless creatures. One of them dove towards her head, getting its claws tangled in her hair. It pulled and tugged, panicking as it tried to free itself, ripping out chunks of hair, while Jenny's screams turned from ones of fear to pain.

A sudden, powerful, and guttural roar came from behind, as Mason's flashlight, bobbing wildly, appeared, briefly illuminating his determined expression as he leapt towards the creatures encircling Jenny. Startled by his appearance, they disentangled themselves from her and hovered above, screeching with anger as Mason punched and kicked at any bat in his reach. His fist connected with one of them, stunning it and leaving it sprawled motionless on the floor. Sensing the odds were against them, the bats turned and flew away, their screeches growing fainter as they headed back towards the gap in the wall.

"Yeah, you better run," Mason bellowed out after them, raising his fists in the air in triumph.

Adam looked down at the bat on the floor and recoiled in disgust. The creature's eyes, one higher than the other, were a disturbing, luminous yellow, and thick pus from their corners ran down its angular face. Its skull was warped, its twisted snout jutting at an unnatural angle as if shaped by something cruel and unseen. Its teeth were jagged and uneven, protruding from its mouth at awkward angles. Two needle-thin fanglike teeth were the exception, standing tall and straight in the center. Bone-like edges on the ends of the thick membrane of its wings gave them a sharp, ragged, and angry appearance. The creature's fur was patchy and matted, revealing slimy, glistening skin beneath. The same foul, sour odor Adam had detected earlier wafted from its body.

"Jesus, you're one ugly son of a bitch aren't you?" Mason said, wrinkling his nose as he caught wind of the animal. He prodded the bat lightly with his foot, then jumped back in surprise as it shifted, its eyes regaining focus and fixing on him. With an ear-piercing screech, the bat regained full control of its senses, gave the group one last baleful look, and got to its feet. Several strong flaps of its wings sent it back into the air, and its silhouette quickly faded back into the darkness as it flew toward the gap where the rest of its colony had already retreated.

"What... What the hell was that?" Adam said, rubbing his temple. "That thing. It just—" He shook his head. "It shouldn't have been able to take off."

Mason frowned in confusion. "What do you mean?"

"Bats push off something when they fly—drop from a ledge, a stalactite, anything. That one—" He swallowed, replaying the way it had moved. "It just... lifted itself off the ground with ease."

A sudden loud thud echoed through the cave, causing Mason and Adam to whip their heads around. Jenny lay sprawled on the ground, panting, her body twisted in an uncomfortable-looking position.

"Hey, are you alright?"

Adam bent to help her sit up, supporting her weight as he eased her back against his chest.

"I... I don't know. I think so," she whispered, her voice trembling with shock.

"Come on, let's get you back to the camp so I can check you out. Um... I mean, check out your wounds."

"Oh, dude," Mason groaned, slapping his forehead and shaking his head.

Despite her predicament, Jenny's lips curved into a smile at Adam's endearing awkwardness, momentarily easing the tension caused by the attack. Her smile was quickly replaced by a grimace and a gasp as a wave of sharp, searing agony pulsed through her wounds.

With the aid of Mason, Adam lifted Jenny up, placing her arm around his shoulder to provide support. Aware of their bodies pressed together, he couldn't escape the conflicting emotions of excitement and guilt, chastising himself for feeling both. Now wasn't the time.

A comforting warmth radiating from the crackling flames of the fire pit near the cave entrance greeted them as the trio approached. Smoke curled lazily through the air, drifting toward the entrance where someone had pulled aside the vines, tying them back to allow the haze to escape. Adam helped Jenny to sit at the base of the cave wall opposite the fire, where she immediately leaned back with a relieved sigh.

"I don't feel great," she said with a whimper, her face appearing pale and weary in the glow of the flickering flames. Her clothing was a patchwork of rips and tears, offering glimpses of the bloody, clawed flesh beneath.

"Okay, let's get you patched up," Adam said, rummaging through his backpack and pulling out a tin box with the iconic medical symbol on it.

"At least someone thought of bringing a first aid kit," Christina said, staring daggers at Jack. She crouched down next to Jenny, intertwining their hands, and gave them a reassuring squeeze.

" I normally do on a hike, but this is a party, and I didn't think we'd need one," Jack said defensively.

His words only served to fuel the fire of Christina's angry glare.

"Hey, how was I supposed to know there was a pack of ravenous bats in here?" Jack exclaimed, raising his arms in surrender.

"Here, let me help," Sarah said, crouching down next to Adam as he pulled out swabs, bandages, and antiseptic cream from the kit, arranging them in preparation to treat Jenny.

"I've got younger brothers, so you could say I'm an expert at first aid."

She shot Adam a warm smile, and they got to work, meticulously cleaning and disinfecting Jenny's wounds before bandaging them.

"Wait, what's this?" Sarah said, her voice filled with concern. Adam secured the bandage around the arm wound he was working on and looked up to see Sarah gazing at a mark on the side of Jenny's neck, running her fingers over it with care.

"Ow!" Jenny said, recoiling from Sarah's touch.

"Sorry," Sarah said, brushing Jenny's hair away from the wound carefully and leaning in for a closer examination. "It looks like a bite mark," she murmured, observing the needle-like puncture wounds near Jenny's jugular. She leaned back and turned her attention to the group. "Hey guys, Jenny has been bitten. I think we'd better head back and get her checked out. Who knows what diseases those bats might have been carrying?"

"Oh man, we only just got set up," Jack huffed, his expression showing his disappointment.

"Jack, we can't just ignore this. Those things weren't just your garden variety bats. They could easily have been carrying some sort of disease."

"Yeah... Yeah, you're right," Jack conceded, a flicker of guilt crossing his face.

"Alright, guys, let's get packed up and…"

"No, it's ok, I'll be fine. I want to stay," Jenny said softly, her eyes flashing with determination.

Everyone turned towards her, their faces displaying varying levels of concern, but Jenny's expression remained resolute. She met each of their eyes, her jaw clenched, as if challenging anyone to oppose her.

"But Jenny… those bats… There was something wrong with them. I really think we should go…" Adam's attempt at persuasion fell flat, his words coming out instead as an uncertain plea.

"I said no, Adam," Jenny said, her lips a thin, tight line as she glared at him before looking away in annoyance.

Christina knelt next to her, searching her eyes.

"Jenny, you already said you don't feel great. We can't risk it. If you get worse…"

"I was just in pain and shocked, is all. I'm feeling much better now that I've been treated. I'll be fine." Her steely gaze brooked no argument.

Christina blew a breath out, her face clouded with doubt. "Well, I guess if you're sure. Just let us know if you start to feel worse, ok?"

Jenny nodded, her lips curling into a thin smile.

A wide grin stretched across Jack's face as he clapped his hands together in gleeful anticipation. "Alright, let's get this party started then," he called out, his voice brimming with enthusiasm, all traces of disappointment erased.

Mason, Jack, Christina, and Sarah each took a can from the open cases of alcohol as Mason set up a Bluetooth speaker. The cave quickly became a cacophony of blaring music and shouting voices as everyone competed to be heard above the noise. Adam studied Jenny with concern. His instincts were screaming at him to get her to Urgent

Care, but he didn't want to force the issue. He watched the others glumly. The last thing he felt like right now was a drink. Despite her obvious disinterest in him, Adam decided he would abstain from partying and focus on making sure Jenny was ok.

Chapter Eleven

On the other side of the gap, concealed deep within the vast cave system, the creature awoke. Its bioluminescent eyes opened wide, and it was immediately bombarded by a barrage of sounds that reverberated in its hyper-sensitive hearing. Its protective instinct engaged as it broke free from the last vestiges of sleep and unfurled its leathery wings to their full ten-foot span, engaging muscles that hadn't been used in years.

Its stomach growled in hunger, its last meal digested and begging once more to be filled. Through its hibernation, it was able to live off its last large meal for forty years, though time had no meaning to it. Not any longer. Its body shuddered with desire, sensing the nearby presence of its favourite meal. This time, it wouldn't have to travel far to get what it needed.

Chapter Twelve
Jack

Jack whooped as he swung Christina around to the beat of the music, their beer cans sloshing their contents onto the rocky ground as they danced. He saw Mason and Sarah were doing the same on the other side of the blazing fire pit.

This was definitely on its way to being the best Halloween party yet. He would need to slow down his drinking a bit, though. He was already three cans in, and he couldn't afford many more if he wanted to perform well on game day. Pulling Christina towards him, he gave her a kiss before breaking away and settling himself down on a rock next to Adam in front of the fire. He glanced between Adam and Jenny, a smirk forming on his face.

Adam was seated on the ground, his eyes searching past the dancing flames to where Jenny remained still, lost in the fire's glow.

"Go on, bro. She looks lonely, go and see if she needs anything," Jack said, leaning toward Adam and slapping him on the shoulder.

Adam's face was already glowing red from the flickering

flames, but Jack could have sworn he turned a shade darker as he adjusted himself awkwardly and shot Jack a quick smile.

Jack's smirk grew as Adam hauled himself to his feet. His grin instantly twisted into one of shock when the rhythmic beat of the music was shattered by the thunderous crash of rocks at the entrance, initiating a cascade of falling debris.

The cavern shook violently, a cloud of grit and rock dust billowing over the stunned group, its chalky smell stinging their noses and making them cough and splutter.

"Oh shit," Jack exclaimed, frantically wiping his face to clear the dust, his widened eyes reflecting his growing panic as he struggled to see through the thick cloud.

"Did the fucking entrance just collapse?" Christina managed to choke out before coughing violently.

With a flashlight in hand and his stomach lurching, Jack brought his shirt up to cover his nose, protecting himself from the dust as he approached the scene of the collapse. As he lifted the vines and directed the flashlight beam to where the entrance should have been, his heart sank. The entrance was now completely blocked by a wall of rocks and boulders. The thickness of the layer of rocks and the unstable-looking roof overhead made it clear that there was no chance of escape in that direction.

"Fuck!" he yelled out, his voice filled with frustration and panic.

"Don't tell me we're trapped in here," Sarah moaned, sniffling from the particles still tickling her nose.

"Does anyone have phone service?" Christina asked, pulling out her phone and squinting at it.

Everyone scrambled for their phones and pulled them out, the resultant muttering of disappointment confirming that no one else had a signal either.

"Well shit," Mason said, his face turning pale as reality sank in.

"Hey, does anyone know we're here? Surely someone will come looking for us, right? I mean, if we're stuck here, that is," Sarah said, looking at the others through the haze.

The room filled with a collective sense of hope as they exchanged glances, but that hope faded into disappointment when no one uttered a word.

"Well, surely someone will come from the DEC, right? I mean, you guys had to get a permit to camp here, didn't you?" Christina said, her eyes locking onto Jack's, searching for confirmation.

Jack's stomach sank with guilt, a cold knot tightening in his chest as he exchanged a look with Mason, their eyes mirroring the same unspoken dread.

"Uhhh, yeah, about that," Jack mumbled, his face flushed with embarrassment as he squirmed and looked away from Christina, suddenly very interested in his shoes.

"You've got to be kidding me!" Christina exclaimed, her hands raised in a mixture of disgust and disbelief. She turned away and stormed deeper into the cave, her footsteps heavy with anger.

"Christina, wait," Jack called out, taking a few steps after her before Sarah grabbed his arm and halted him.

"Let her go. She needs to cool off. We need to work out what we're going to do."

Jack sighed, his eyes downcast as he wiped beads of muddy sweat from his forehead, giving a weary nod.

"Hey, what about that gap at the back of the cave?" Adam asked.

The group stared at him in silence before a collective sigh of relief rippled through the air, breaking the tension.

"Shit, you're right. That gap is just big enough to fit through. Of course, it will be a tighter squeeze for some than others, but we should all make it," Jack said with optimism.

"Wait... What about Jenny?" Adam asked.

The group's attention shifted, their gazes drawn to Jenny, still seated across from the murky haze of the fire's glow.

"I'll be OK," Jenny said. "I just might need a bit of a push, is all," she added with a pained chuckle as she rose to her feet with some difficulty, giving the group a faint smile.

After a quick search for their scattered flashlights and retrieving the few they found, Sarah and Adam hung back to help Jenny while Jack led them all towards the back of the cave where Christina had headed.

Jack knew that had he contacted the DEC, the cave would undoubtedly have been declared off-limits, so he made the decision not to. Mason had gone along with him as he always did. There was no way the girls would have agreed to come if they knew. Now he could only hope that the gap he'd found would lead to a way out or at least to a place where they could get a bar of reception.

A hush fell over the group as they ventured deeper into the cave, with only the sound of their footsteps reverberating around them until a shrill scream pierced the air. Jack's heart began to race. It was emanating from the direction Christina had been heading, right in front of them.

Chapter Thirteen
Christina

Seething with anger, Christina left the glow of the campfire behind, ignoring Jack's calls for her to come back. How could he have been so irresponsible? And Mason, too? Jack had always been reckless, but never to this extent. She probably should have expected it to elevate to something rash sooner or later, though. Lately, he had been more cocksure and arrogant than usual, and she was beginning to tire of it. She flicked on her flashlight as she rounded the corner and swung the beam around, scanning the walls and the path before her. She had seen the gap Jack had discovered, but maybe there had been other passages or gaps he had missed along the way.

The air here was rich with the scent of earth and minerals, a blend of moss and damp stone mingling together with a hint of something wild and untamed. She took the opportunity to breathe it in, trying to clear the dust from her airways before she continued.

The ridges and grooves of the cave walls began to close in on her as she approached the end of the cave where the gap was. The torchlight began to reflect off the damp walls like scattered diamonds in the dark. Velvety moss patches revealed themselves, softening the harsh edges of the rock walls and adding a touch of life to the otherwise stark environment.

As hard as she looked, she didn't discover any other passages or gaps more than a few inches wide besides the one she now stood before. She studied the gap, her anxiety rising with each sweep of the flashlight. The opening was smaller than she thought it had been.

She stepped forward, sticking her head cautiously through, and swept the flashlight along both sides of the walls. There were areas of jagged rock that could easily snag clothing or do worse damage if the person going through wasn't careful. At the very end, where the gap ended, darkness awaited. It appeared as though it could lead to another cave or passage beyond, but for all she knew, it could lead to an impassable crevice. "There's only one way to find out," she muttered to herself.

Taking a deep breath, she edged herself sideways into the gap, the arm holding the flashlight extended ahead of her. Despite her fears, the going was relatively easy. Her clothing caught only a few times, but she managed to disentangle herself without causing any tears. She was roughly at the halfway point when she heard the familiar flutter of wings accompanied by an angry screech.

A wave of fear froze her in place, making her arm holding the flashlight shake violently as the image of the bat tangled in Jenny's hair flooded into her mind.

She began to slowly inch herself back the way she came. She was so distracted by the sounds ahead of her that she didn't realise when the back of her shirt got caught on an outcropping until she went to move and found that she couldn't.

"Oh fuck," she whispered before she clamped her lips

shut, hoping that the already agitated bats hadn't heard. The angry screech and rush of air approaching her changed that hope to panic. Abandoning all attempts at stealth, she yanked herself back toward the entrance to no avail, her movement only serving to bunch up more of the fabric of her shirt on the outcropping.

"Help!" she screamed in desperation, as she threw herself once more toward the entrance, hearing a slight tear but yelping as her skin caught the sharp edge. Pain exploded through her lower back as she repeatedly strained against the fabric, a tug of war turned bloody as her flesh grated against the unforgiving rock.

Suddenly, she felt something sharp land on her head before pulling away, her long blond tresses lifting into the air as they wrapped themselves around the screeching bat's feet.

Her terrified screams were deafening in the small gap, serving only to increase the bat's agitation. She continued to try to pull herself away from the rock, each attempt ripping a larger hole in her shirt, but not enough to disengage from it.

"Christina!" Jack's powerful voice boomed from the entrance. "Grab onto my hand!"

Her hand instinctively reached for his as the bat wrenched at her hair, yanking her head back with it. Screaming in pain, she felt Jack's hand find hers, and she was pulled with a forceful tug toward him. Her shirt tore free, taking with it some of her flesh as she continued to scream. The bat was dragged along with her, its claws still entangled within a thick clump of her hair.

The next thing she knew, she was out and in Jack's arms as Mason whirled and punched at the screeching creature above her. Twisting and turning, it finally freed itself and flew back through the gap, taking a few strands of her hair with it.

Jack knelt, taking her full weight as he held her in his arms and rocked her. The rhythmic movement was a counterpoint to her shuddering sobs and trembling body as her forehead pressed against his chest.

Her breaths, shallow and rapid, barely filled her lungs as they passed through her quivering lips. Her heart hammered in a frantic rhythm against her ribcage, a stark contrast to the slow-motion of reality around her. Shock enveloped her like a heavy fog, temporarily obscuring the events that had just occurred. Time seemed to stretch and contract, seconds feeling like hours, her sense of reality slipping through her fingers like sand.

"Baby, hey, you're ok. I'm here, everything is fine. You're safe."

Gradually coming back to her senses, the searing pain in her back hit her like a wave, making her hiss and arch her back in agony.

"Everything is fine? Are you fucking kidding me?" Christina yelled, her voice sharp and laced with fury, her body stiffening in response.

A fresh wave of agony swept through her at her movement. It felt like every nerve in her back was on fire. It was a pain so intense, so sharp, it stole her breath and made her vision swim. She cried out and sobbed, desperate for some respite from the needle-like pain emanating from the wounds.

"Get out of the way, idiot," Sarah said, shoving a gawking Mason to the side so she could get past, carrying what remained of the first aid kit. "Lay her down gently on her chest and step back," she told Jack.

Every movement Jack made intensified the agony in

Christina's back, a protest that felt amplified a hundredfold, and her throat was raw from screaming. Someone laid down a jacket for her to rest her head on, and an eternity later, at least it felt that way to her, she was settled on the ground.

"Adam, I could use your help here," Sarah said, the nervous hitch in her voice betraying how bad the wound actually was.

"Oh god," Adam said as he crouched down beside Sarah.

Christina could hear him dry retching, which sent her panic levels rising straight to the roof.

"Honey, this is going to hurt a lot, but it needs to be done, you know that, right?"

Christina nodded gingerly.

"Ok, here goes," Sarah said with a hissing breath.

Christina could hear the top being unscrewed from a vodka bottle along with the sloshing of its contents before all she knew was pain and then, nothing.

Chapter Fourteen
Jack

As the last of the bandages was put in place, Jack stroked Christina's sweat-soaked hair one last time before he stood up and stretched with a groan.

Sarah and Adam gave him a disgusted look as they packed up. They had used all of the bandages, and the antiseptic cream tube was almost empty, with only a quarter left. From here, they had to hope there would be no further need for any first aid. Despite the events of the past few hours, Jack was confident. He had to be. He refused to be anything else. There was a faint breeze coming from the gap, which could only mean air was getting in somewhere. If air was flowing in, then they could get out, or at least get close enough to the surface to get a phone signal.

He looked down at Christina sorrowfully. Guilt gnawed at his insides, a relentless ache that refused to be ignored. If only he had been more careful pulling her from the gap, her wound wouldn't have been so bad. But if he had, then who knew what damage the bat would have eventually done? As it was, her entire lower back had been torn to shreds. Strips of skin had been pulled loose, hanging by the thinnest pieces of flesh. It was like she had been savaged by a bear. The bandages, despite being several layers deep, were already stained with blood. Her shirt was ruined and covered in holes on the back, small ones on the front.

He approached the gap, hoping to shield his self-pity from the view of the others. All he had wanted was for tonight to be special, to be an escape from the pressures of college and football that had been getting to him more and more. But he knew he'd been selfish and more than a little reckless. Lately, he'd just felt like he was drowning and all he wanted was to come up for air. The only way he'd found to combat that feeling was to do spontaneous things that excited him. Problem was, he'd been thinking only of himself and not the consequences of what his actions might do to others. Now his love lay face down on the ground, comatose, a victim of his stupidity.

The weight of his failures pressed down on him, but he forced himself back to the present. This was no time to be dwelling on things. He needed to find a way to get them out of this mess he had made, to redeem himself in some small way at least.

He aimed his flashlight through the gap and grimaced when he saw the strips of fabric and blood on the outcropping he had pulled Christina free from. Forcing himself to look beyond it, he could only see darkness. The chittering noises from the bats that had been there had fallen silent. He could only hope that they had been scared away by Christina's screams. There was nothing for it. He had to try to make it through himself to see what awaited them.

"Mason, take this and keep it focused ahead of me. I'm going to go through and see what's on the other side." He handed Mason his flashlight and gave him a nod before turning back to the gap.

"Are you crazy?" Sarah snapped, looking at him incredulously.

"Christina is lying here injured, and you decide to try to go through the gap that tore her back to shreds?"

"We have no choice, Sarah," Jack said with a heavy sigh. "There's nowhere else to go. Through there is the only option," he said, pointing at the gap. Plus, it sounds like those bats are gone now. It's the best opportunity I might have. Mason, keep that flashlight steady, ok?"

"Yes, boss," Mason said, forcing a smile.

Sarah huffed and turned away, crossing her arms in disgust.

With the flashlight trained on the gap, Jack edged himself inside. He had barely gotten a few steps in before he found himself scraping against the rocks on both sides.

"Oh fuck," Jack muttered to himself. He paused for a moment to take a breath, feeling his heart begin to pound. He could feel cold trickles of sweat running down his back and forming on his brow despite the chilly air.

Resuming his journey, he winced as he felt his shirt catch on the rocks as he progressed, causing the fabric to rip and tear at regular intervals. Stopping just before the outcropping of rock that had snagged Christina, he peered into the darkness ahead nervously.

"Hey, Mason, lift the flashlight above me, will you? I can't see anything ahead," he called out.

"Alright, but hurry it up, I can't keep holding the flashlight up like this for long. My shoulders are my weakest body part," Mason said jokingly.

"Sarah would say otherwise, but I'll try my best," Jack couldn't resist retorting.

"He's right, you know," he heard Sarah say to Mason, her earlier anger at him apparently having faded enough to inject a bit of humour into a dire situation.

"Hey!" Mason said, the flashlight glow disappearing from the gap, leaving Jack in complete darkness.

"Mason, concentrate, will you? I can't see shit in here," Jack snapped in annoyance.

"Yeah, well, maybe don't provoke the guy with the light, huh? And hurry it up. My shoulders ARE my weakest body part," Mason yelled back, the flashlight's glow illuminating the way ahead of Jack once more.

Jack shook his head and smiled thinly. Studying the outcropping and its location, he decided to try to crouch and crab walk underneath it. There was scarcely enough room between his knees and the wall, but he managed to get low enough for his head to pass beneath. With some difficulty, he inched past it and straightened up again. Wiping the sweat away from his eyes, he took the opportunity to look ahead. To his relief, the rest of the way, while still arduous, seemed to be snag-free. Gripping the wall with his hand extended in front of him, he found he was able to pull himself through quicker. Finally, his hand stretched out into freedom, and he wrapped it around the wall and pulled himself toward the exit. He paused there and reached into his pocket for his phone, activating the flashlight function. He swept the beam across the floor, hoping for a solid surface rather than a bottomless crevasse. Relief washed over him when he spotted the cavern floor, and he pulled himself through the gap into the open air of the cavern before him. He leant against the wall and sucked in breaths as he waited for his heart to return to its natural rhythm.

"Jack? Are you dead?" Mason's distant voice called out nervously behind him, the faint glow of the flashlight beam sweeping up and down through the gap.

"Lucky for you, I'm not. You'd never make it through life if I were," Jack shouted back with a smile. He held up his phone and swept the beam around him. This cavern appeared much larger than the one he had come from. The walls on the opposite side of where he was remained in darkness, the flashlight on his phone not strong enough to illuminate them.

"OK, you can come back now," Mason called out. "We need to figure out what to do with Christina and Jenny."

"Oh shit," Jack mumbled to himself. He recalled the difficulty he had in making it through the gap. Going back was the last thing he wanted to do, and then having to come back through again afterwards? It would be better to stay where he was. The best thing he could do for both Christina and Jenny was to find a way out or find a place with phone reception.

"Hey guys, I'm going to stay here," he called back through the gap. "I'll search for a way out and get help. I'll be back as soon as I can."

Silence met his ears, broken only by the faint, echoing voices from the other side of the gap, their muffled words bouncing off the rough stone walls as he examined the cavern.

The ground before him was a patchwork of fresh and dried bat guano, the creatures themselves nowhere to be seen—no doubt driven into the depths by the group's commotion. Beyond, scattered rocks lay in silent witness to time, their surfaces draped in moss and lichen, a testament to their long, undisturbed presence.

A faint splash of water drew his attention to the middle of the cave, where there was a rocky bowl-shaped formation. He directed the beam to the roof, where a group of stalactites had formed, the largest one the source of the dripping water that was adding to the pool's crystalline surface beneath it. Like the stalactite above it, the pool of water seemed almost alive in the dim light of the phone's flashlight. It was shimmering with a subtle, almost ethereal bluish glow from the minerals that fed it. It was hard to pull his gaze away from.

The rest of the cave, visible in the limited light, was a chaotic jumble of rising and falling rock formations. His heart pounded with excitement and renewed hope as he saw an unknown source of light illuminating a distant part of the cave, beyond the reach of his phone's flashlight.

He was just about to head in that direction when Mason's loud shout came through the gap behind him, reverberating through the cave.

Chapter Fifteen
Sarah

"Wait, Sarah and I are coming with you," Mason called out.

Sarah stared at him increculously from where she was seated on the ground.

"What the fuck are you doing? We just discussed this. We can't just leave Christina here, and Jenny is in no condition to come with us either," she hissed, gesturing at the girls.

Christina was still unconscious and lying on her chest, Jack's bunched-up jacket positioned underneath her forehead. Jenny was sitting nearby against the wall, her ragged breathing a clear sign to all except for Mason that she was also not doing so well.

"C'mon, we can't just let Jack go by himself. Besides, Adam already volunteered to stay behind and watch out for them." He looked toward Adam pointedly, daring him to say otherwise.

"Y... Yeah, that's right. Happy to stay behind here. You guys go. If you guys find separate passages in there, you'll need people to investigate them to save time. The sooner you find an exit and get help, the better it will be for the girls," Adam said, searching Mason's eyes for a hint of approval.

"I can't believe what I'm hearing," Sarah muttered, not wanting to admit Adam was right but knowing he was. She just really didn't want to leave the girls behind. She met Mason's determined gaze with her own and sighed. Once he got an idea in his mind, especially when it came to supporting Jack, it was almost impossible to change it. "Fine, I guess what Adam said makes sense," she muttered. She looked at Adam, feeling uncertainty flood through her. She didn't know Adam that well. He was always hanging around Jack and Mason, and he had a habit of disappearing when the girls were with them. She'd only heard second-hand stories of him, and what she'd heard didn't exactly fill her with reassurance. He seemed more of a follower than a leader.

"Are you sure you can look after them if something goes wrong?"

Shifting uneasily, Adam briefly glanced at her before returning his attention to the girls. "Well, we've already used pretty much all the first aid stuff we have now. We only have a quarter tube of antiseptic, a handful of painkillers, and a few swabs left, so it's not like you could do much more anyway." He turned his face to the ground as he spoke, his expression unreadable. "I'll be ok with them. Just go get help as quickly as you can, yeah?" he said, his eyes flicking between Mason and her with a nervous look of trepidation on his face.

Sarah absorbed his words and nodded, studying his face. His demeanour didn't exactly evoke confidence, but he was right. There wasn't much she could do even if she did stay. It would be best for all of them if they could find help ASAP. "OK," she said, nodding in resignation.

Mason nodded at Sarah, a half-smile on his face, before he turned back toward the gap. "Just wait there, Sarah and I are going to grab the backpacks and come through."

A momentary silence was broken by the distant voice of Jack. "OK, grab mine too while you're there."

"Was always the plan, bro, I'm stupid but not that stupid," he muttered to himself, a wry smile on his face. "Come on, babe, let's hurry back and get this show on the road," he said, extending his hand out for Sarah to take. Sarah put her hand in his and, with his help, pulled herself to her feet.

"We'll grab your backpack, too, Adam. We'll leave you guys with enough supplies to last while we get help," Sarah said reassuringly.

Adam nodded, the flashlight he'd placed on the ground to illuminate the cave casting grim shadows on his face, almost as if it was reflecting the reality of their predicament.

Sarah followed Mason back down the tunnel toward the entrance, following the torchlight cast before them in silence. As they rounded the corner ahead of them, the fire pit came into view, now a pile of smoking embers that made their surroundings seem more ominous. The coiled vines lying amongst the rubble at the entrance appeared snakelike in the dim lighting, and Sarah found herself shivering. A sense of foreboding and unease flew down her spine, raising goosebumps on her arms and sending shivers through her body. The air felt heavy and still, adding to her unease. It wasn't until now that she felt the reality of the dire situation they were in. Their only hope lay in finding a way out through the caves—but whether one even existed remained a terrifying unknown. The likelihood felt slim. The chilling possibilities started swirling in her mind, a tide of "what ifs," but she consciously pulled herself back to the immediate moment. This was no time to fall apart. The girls were relying on her, Mason, and Jack to find a way out. She drew in a breath to compose herself, capturing Mason's attention, who looked at her curiously.

"Everything alright? Wait... No, that's a stupid question, of course it isn't," he said, moving closer to her and throwing an arm around her shoulders, drawing her to him.

Feeling the beginning of tears forming in the corners of her eyes, she struggled to answer him past the sudden lump in her throat. "I'm scared, Mason. I'm barely holding it together, but I have to. Christina and Jenny are counting on us, but I'm terrified. What if we don't find anything on the other side of the gap? What if it's just one large cavern with nowhere else to go?" Her body shook as she fought to contain the flood of emotion, but it was a losing battle.

"Hey... Hey. It's ok, we'll work something out. We don't know what's in that cavern. For all we know, Jack has already found some passages or something while we've been away. We just need to focus on what we can do right now, yeah? We'll work out the rest when we get there." His tender voice brought her back to earth a bit. It had a tendency to do that. Despite how goofy and clueless he acted on the outside, those closest to him knew better.

It was the playfulness, his boyish good looks, carefree attitude, and sense of humour that had first attracted her to him. Of course, his sport-hardened body didn't hurt either. To her surprise, when they started dating, she saw the reality behind the façade he had created. That sensitive, caring, and strong man was the one she had fallen for, and those same qualities were being displayed here in her hour of need. Her rock, underneath the massive rock they found themselves in, she thought to herself, coaxing a whisper of a smile to her face through the tears.

"Yeah, ok," she murmured, savouring the last moments of his comforting hug before she pulled away to compose herself and wipe at her eyes. "Alright, let's grab what we need," she said, eyeing the pile of backpacks and sleeping bags near the cave wall beside the collapsed entrance. "Do we need to take the sleeping bags too, just in case?"

"No, I think we leave them," Mason said, rubbing his chin thoughtfully. "I mean, it's going to be a pain lugging both around if there's going to be more tight scrapes. We'll be out of here before we need them anyway," he said, throwing her a smile.

"Let's hope you're right," Sarah said.

Mason started sorting through the backpacks and retrieved his before handing Sarah hers.

"Wait," Sarah said. "We need to organise our supplies and make sure we leave enough for Adam and the girls."

Mason nodded in agreement, and together, the pair sorted through the backpacks, separating the supplies in two. Mason, Sarah, and Jack would take half of the snacks but would leave extra water bottles behind for Adam and the girls. They placed the snacks for the trio being left behind into one of the spare backpacks and filled Adam's with water bottles. If she, Mason, and Jack ran out of water, there was the possibility of finding a source on their journey. Adam and the girls didn't have that luxury, being stuck where they were.

"OK, I think we're set," Sarah said, double-checking the amounts before repacking her, Jack's, and Mason's backpacks.

They picked up their backpacks and threw them over their shoulders, Mason taking Jack's by its straps.

"Jack's probably left us behind by now," Mason said, shifting anxiously as he waited for Sarah to take the lead with her flashlight.

"Not everything is about him, you know," Sarah snapped as the pair headed down the corridor back towards the gap. "In fact, if you and Jack had applied for a permit like you should have done, we wouldn't be in as much of a mess as we are right now."

"I know," Mason said, his shoulders slumping in response. "I'm sorry, baby. Jack and I have done some stupid things in the past, but this takes the cake, hey?" his voice, heavy with defeat, whispered forlornly.

Instantly, she began to regret what she'd said. This situation was tough on everyone. Yes, the boys should have gotten the permit, but there was little they could do about it now. There was no use adding to the tension of the situation; it wouldn't solve anything.

"Well, it wasn't one of your smartest ideas," she said, toning down the aggression in her voice.

"I swear I'll make it up to you," he said, the beginnings of a mischievous smile forming on his face in the shadows. "How about we go on a vacation when we get out of here, somewhere warm and sunny with a beach? We can drink as much as we want, swim as much as we want, take day trips..." he snickered, turning his gaze to her body and scanning it up and down. "Or just spend the day in bed where I'll be your sex slave."

"You're an idiot," she said with a laugh, her face softening with amusement. "First of all, we need to get out of here; then we need to concentrate on graduating. Oh, and there's also the fact that you're flat broke and you can barely afford to buy me dinner as it is."

"Sarah, don't let reality get in the way of dreams. You have to think big. You know, like the size of my..." he gestured towards his crotch, his goofiness now on full display.

Sarah gave him a push in faux disgust, feeling her tension and anger subside as she giggled. "You're such a romantic, you know that?" she said, shaking her head as Mason's laughter echoed around them.

"A romantic? You can't mean Mason then," a weak disembodied voice said from in front of them.

"Christina?" Sarah called, feeling relief sweep through her.

The pair rounded the corner of the narrowing corridor to see Christina rolled onto her side, her head still resting on Jack's bunched-up jacket. She raised a hand over her eyes to shield herself from the glow of Sarah's flashlight as it fell on the pair.

"It's about time you woke up," Sarah said with a smile.

"Yeah, well, if someone didn't make me pass out, I wouldn't have needed to," Christina retorted with an answering smile of her own. "Thank you, by the way. For fixing me up."

"Girl, you're far from fixed up. You need a doctor, stat," Sarah said, trying to keep her voice light. "That's why we're heading through the gap to meet Jack and see if we can get out of here and get you two girls some help."

Christina nodded, a grim look on her face.

Sarah looked toward Jenny, who was still seated on the ground, back against the wall in the same position as when they had left to gather the supplies. She walked over and crouched beside her, studying Jenny's face with growing concern. In the short time they'd been gone, her condition seemed to have worsened. Her skin was pale and waxy with a sheen of sweat coating it despite the chill in the air. Her eyes were ringed in darkness, and her breathing was short and shallow. Performing a check of the bandages and plaster placed on Jenny's wounds, Sarah could see some were stained with blood, but there was little she could do about that now, given they had no bandages left. The puncture mark near Jenny's neck made Sarah particularly concerned. The surrounding skin was puffy and inflamed, pointing to an infection of some kind. Sarah forced a smile onto her face and looked at Jenny, meeting her eyes with her own.

"How are you doing, Jenny?"

"Not... Not good," Jenny managed to say between breaths. Involuntary shivers passed through her body. "I feel... cold and hot at the same time. That's... not a good sign... is it?" she said, a pained smile twisting her lips.

"You'll be ok. Jack, Mason, and I will be back with help soon, and we'll get you all fixed up. Just hang in there, yeah? I'm sure Adam here will look after you, won't you, Adam?" Her eyes, cold and hard as steel, met Adam's; a nervous smile flickered across his lips in response.

"Yeah, I've got this. I'll make sure you girls are well looked after," Adam said, his expression softening as he looked at Jenny.

Oh god, Sarah thought to herself. *He's really got it bad for her. But hey, maybe that's not a bad thing right now when she needs all the help she can get.*

"We'd better get going," Mason said, shuffling anxiously, obviously eager to get moving.

"Yeah, yeah, we can't let your boyfriend wait too long," she said with a smirk.

After a final round of goodbyes, Mason launched Sarah's backpack through the gap to the other side and did the same with his own and Jack's.

Giving the girls one last look, Sarah squeezed into the gap behind Mason, hoping beyond measure that they would find a way to get the help they so desperately needed.

Chapter Sixteen
Jack

"OK, grab mine too while you're there," Jack called back.

He couldn't help but feel a sense of relief when he heard that Mason and Sarah were coming. Despite his outward display of machismo, inside, he was filled with uncertainty and fear about what lay ahead. Was there a way out of here, or had he brought doom upon them all?

He pushed aside his worries and decided to do a cursory exploration of the cave while he waited for Mason and Sarah.

The glow from his phone barely pushed back against the suffocating blackness ahead, its light swallowed whole by the yawning void, as if the darkness itself had an insatiable hunger.

With a deep breath, Jack began to walk towards the middle of the cavern. With each footstep he took, echoing off the ancient stone walls, he stepped around the rocks littering the floor carefully. The air was cool and damp, carrying the faint scent of earth and minerals.

Shadows danced on the walls, flickering and shifting

with every movement of his phone. The cavern was vast and far larger than he had first thought. Its ceiling soared high above, decorated with jagged stalactites jutting out from the darkness, hanging over him like the teeth of some primordial beast.

The ground beneath his feet was uneven, a mosaic of rocks and stones that crunched softly with each step. Venturing past the rock bowl pool of stalactite water, he kept heading toward the seemingly unending darkness ahead of him. After a few more minutes of walking, he still couldn't see the other side.

Gradually, a faint semblance of light began to emanate before him, becoming clearer the nearer he drew, revealing itself to be the glint of minerals embedded in the rock high above the wall near the ceiling, sparkling like stars in the night. The light he'd first seen originated from this, dashing the small hope it had offered.

Shrugging it off, he continued. This cavern was so large; there had to be an exit somewhere. It was clear that it would take a decent chunk of time to explore, and now, more than ever, he was glad for Sarah and Mason's imminent arrival.

All of a sudden, a faint whisper of wind brushed past him, hardly more than a sigh. Alarmed, his thoughts turned toward the bats that had attacked the group earlier, and he swivelled around to face its origin. He scanned the area with his phone flashlight, but its source proved elusive. Whatever it had been was gone, or at least beyond his limited vision.

It was then, as he held his phone up and his eyes caught the screen display, that panic began to set in.

"Oh shit," he muttered loudly, startling even himself in the eerie silence of the cave. His phone battery was sitting at 13%. He cursed himself silently. He knew he should have charged it before coming, but in the excitement of organizing the trip, he had forgotten to. Being a second-hand phone and several generations old, its battery did not hold up like it used to. He usually had to recharge it once or more during the day to ensure it lasted until evening.

Somehow, in all the chaos of the day's events, the fact that their phones would eventually run out of battery hadn't even touched his mind. A reality that was now literally staring him in the face.

"Oh fuck," he muttered as another unwelcome thought wormed its way into his brain.

It wasn't only the phones that would run out of battery, but the flashlights they had brought, too. The gravity of their situation began to sink in, and he realized that they were in bigger trouble than any of them had recognized or at least voiced to each other.

"Goddamn it guys, hurry the fuck up," he said once more out loud, his voice bouncing around the cave, amplifying in the confined space.

Suddenly, a piercing shriek cut through the air. Jack's heart stopped as he froze in place, stiff with shock. The sound was otherworldly, a chilling cry that seemed to come from the very depths of the earth. It reverberated through the cavern, and he felt a creeping dread settle in. The shriek was unlike anything he had ever heard, a mix of anger and pain that echoed with an eerie resonance. He felt a cold sweat break out on his forehead as he forced himself to stand still, his every instinct screaming at him to run.

The cave seemed to hold its breath, the silence pregnant with tension. Jack strained to listen; his senses heightened by fear. The darkness around him felt more oppressive, the shadows deeper and more menacing. He could almost feel the presence of the unknown creature, lurking just beyond the reach of his phone's light.

His mind raced with possibilities, each one more terrifying than the last. What the hell kind of creature could make such a sound? And was it coming closer? His legs were heavy with tension and rooted to the spot. At this point, he couldn't run even if he wanted to.

He swallowed hard, trying to steady his nerves. The shriek had faded, but its echo lingered in his mind, a haunting reminder of the cave's hidden dangers. Taking deep breaths, his pulse began to return to its natural rhythm as the minutes passed by with no further sound. "F..." he began to say, but caught himself at the last moment. He had to warn Mason and Sarah before they came face-to-face with its source.

Chapter Seventeen
Sarah

"Ok, so surprisingly, you've made it through with only a few small rips in your shirt and jeans," Sarah said as she finished her inspection.

"To be honest, I'm kinda disappointed that you don't have any," Mason said, letting his eyes rove over Sarah's body.

"Lucky, I don't. I hardly have any material on me as it is," she giggled.

"You'll have even less on you soon if I get my way," Mason said, reaching out to grab her around the waist.

"Typical Mason, always thinking with your downstairs brain, even in life-or-death situations," she said, twisting out of the way to avoid his hands.

"Well, you can't blame a guy for trying," he said with a lascivious grin.

"Guys!" hissed a voice through the darkness. Startled, Sarah spun and swung her flashlight wildly around them. The way the cavern carried sound made it difficult to determine where any sound source came from.

"You have to be quiet. There's something in here with

us, something that sounds really pissed off." Jack stepped into the glow of Sarah's flashlight, a look of fear on his face that sent her stomach into tight knots. She'd never seen Jack afraid before, and the way he looked over his shoulder in panic filled her with dread.

"Fuck dude, you scared the shit out of me," Mason said in his typical laid back manner, not paying attention to Jacks' words.

"Shut the fuck up," Jack hissed at him as he joined them. "I'm telling you, we have to be quiet. I think I pissed something off and whatever it is sounded big."

"What should we do then, bro?" Mason said, finally lowering his voice to a whisper.

"We can't just sit here and do nothing; we need to find a way out," Sarah whispered. "Jenny and Christina are in a bad way. We need to get help ASAP," she added.

The group was silent for a moment. It was a simple decision as far as Sarah was concerned. Even if what Jack said was true, and she had no reason to believe it wasn't, they still had to find a way out. They would just have to be quiet and extra vigilant.

Jack blew out his breath slowly and gave a single nod. "OK, yeah, you're right. But guys, we seriously need to be quiet from here on. Keep your eyes open wherever you go. Who knows what the fuck is in here with us." He hesitated before adding, "Listen, we also need to try to conserve our batteries, too, both on our phones and flashlights. We don't know how long it's going to take to find a way out of here and we're fucked if we don't have light."

His words sent a chill down Sarah's spine. She doubted anyone, herself included, had considered the batteries. It brought even more urgency to what they needed to do.

"How do you propose we do that, bro? It's not like we can walk around in the darkness," Mason said, a hint of frustration on his face. His tendency to voice his thoughts without thinking was usually entertaining, but right at this moment, Sarah wished he would just shut up.

"Switch between using your flashlight and phone, Mason. Use your head for once," Sarah snapped, feeling her tension rise to an all-time high. "Can we just get on with it? We don't have time to waste," she said.

Jack nodded and pointed in the direction he had come from. "I didn't have a chance to check out the area where I was properly before that thing frightened the shit out of me," he said, keeping his volume low. "I'll go back that way. Mason, you follow the walls around to the right. Sarah, you take the left. Clear?"

"Got it, boss," Mason said, shooting a sheepish apologetic glance at Sarah.

Sarah nodded, pointedly ignoring Mason in favour of turning toward the cave wall to the left. She was in no mood to talk things out with him. They all needed to focus on the task at hand.

Suddenly, the horrifying realization that she'd forgotten Adam's backpack slammed into her like a physical blow. She had been so panicked and focused on what she and Mason needed that, despite separating the supplies, she had failed to notice that neither of them had brought it along with them.

"Ah, shit!" she hissed, a cold wave of guilt and panic washing over her, constricting her chest. Regret gnawed at her, a bitter taste filling her mouth, but there wasn't much she could do about it now. Hopefully, Adam would realize in time and go and retrieve it and anything else they needed. With a few deep, centering breaths, she stilled the racing thoughts in her head. What's done was done; she needed now to focus on finding a way out of there for all of them.

As the other two went their separate ways, she scanned

the area ahead of her. Her path looked to be blocked at several points by large rockfalls, which she'd have to navigate around, but otherwise, there was nothing of note to see. She began walking; each step was deliberate, her eyes scanning the wall for any sign of a passage.

A few minutes later, her torchlight fell on something ahead of her, setting her pulse racing. It was a small pile of bones scattered near the base of the wall. She knelt next to them, the scene bathed in her flashlight's beam. The bones were bleached white, their shapes twisted and broken. She examined them, hoping fervently that they were not human. She shuddered at the thought. There was no way they could be, surely. There had been no sign of anyone else being in this cavern or the one they had come from up to now. Although she had to admit, this cavern was huge, and she had only seen a small portion of it. There could just as easily have been some other signs in a part of the cave they hadn't discovered yet.

She shook that thought off and rose to her feet, continuing along her path next to the wall. The cavern seemed to stretch endlessly, its secrets hidden in the shadows beyond the light of her flashlight. Suddenly, she felt a faint breeze brush against her face, cool and refreshing. The draft was coming from ahead of her, a subtle but unmistakable sign of an opening.

Her pulse quickened as she followed the breeze, her flashlight guiding the way. There, it fell upon an unmistakable patch of darkness, a gap between the walls. A passage! The cool air flowed from it, carrying with it hope and the possibility of rescue.

She swung around and opened her mouth to call out to the guys when she remembered Jack's warning. She looked around for the telltale glow of flashlights, only to see there were two of them in the same location across the other side of the cave.

"What the fuck are they doing?" she whispered to herself.

Hoping to attract their attention, she swept her flashlight beam back and forth, only to discover their flashlights were doing the same. It looked like another passage had been discovered by either Mason or Jack, prompting the other to join and check it out.

Shit," she muttered. They should have discussed what to do in the event of one of them finding a passage. Frustrated by the continual signalling of the flashlights on the other side, she decided to leave hers there to mark her location and use her phone to guide her to the other side.

She placed the flashlight on the ground, thumbed on the flashlight function on her phone, and began to make her way toward them.

A few minutes later, she could hear the hushed whispers of the two boys as she neared them.

"Guys, keep it down, remember? Sound carries easily in this cavern."

"Sarah, look, I found a passage," came Mason's excited voice as he tried to keep his volume down.

She reached the two boys, who were crouched down and shining their flashlight into a gap in the cave wall at the base. It appeared to be large enough to crawl through on hands and knees. As she crouched down, she could feel warmth emanate from the opening. Then a scent hit her suddenly, a foul, acrid odor that clung to the air and seemed to seep into her very pores and made her wrinkle her nose in disgust.

"Fuck, what's that smell?" she managed to say, breathing in through her mouth to try to avoid retching.

"Yeah, it's pretty rich," Jack agreed. "But I don't see any

other choice but to go through anyway. I didn't find a damn thing besides a bunch of bat shit."

"Well, I did," Sarah said, standing up and stepping away from the passage to get some fresh air.

"You did?" Mason asked excitedly.

"I was trying to signal to you guys, but you were doing the same, didn't you see me?"

"We thought you were signalling back to say you understood," Jack said.

"Of course you did," Sarah muttered. "Anyway, I left the flashlight on over there so we could find it again." She indicated the flashlight, still focused on the wall where she had left it.

"Fuck yeah, that's awesome babe," Mason said as he moved toward her to do his signature pick up and spin manoeuvre.

"Now's not the time," Sarah said, warding off his hands with a thin smile.

"Alright, yeah, totally," Mason said, raising his arms up in a show of peace, a wide smile on his face. "So, what do we do now? Which passage do we take?" he asked, glancing between Jack and Sarah.

"Well, mine you can walk through, and there's a fresh cool breeze coming from it, unlike this one which is warm and smells like shit," she said wrinkling her nose as she glanced at the hole in disgust. "I know which one I'd prefer."

"Yeah, but how do we know if that's the one that will lead us out of here? For all we know, it could be this one," Jack said.

He was right, Sarah realized. No matter how small the likelihood was that the passage Mason had found was the one to get them out of here, she couldn't discount the possibility.

"Maybe we ought to split up and take both passages," she said quietly. Despite knowing it was the best option, she knew there were risks involved. Anything could go wrong in here. Another cave collapse, someone getting wedged in a tight gap in a passage, another bat encounter, or coming face to face with whatever made the mysterious screech that Jack heard—all were genuine possibilities.

"What? No way, we should just take one and stick together," Mason protested.

"Mason, we can't. We have to find a way out. There's three of us, so I say one of us can take one passage and the other two take the other."

Jack nodded slowly, "Yeah, I think you're probably right." He straightened up and looked toward the passage nearby. "OK, I'll take this one, you guys take the other. Should we meet back here in an hour?"

"No, I don't think we can afford to," Sarah said quietly. "I think we just need to find a way out and get help. If one of us finds that our way is blocked, then we can come back here and go down the other passage. Otherwise, I say we keep going and find a way through. Whoever does can get help."

"But what if we get lost? How do we know how big this place is?" Mason asked, a frown etched on his face.

"We don't, babe, but it's a risk we have to take," Sarah said.

The group stood in silence for a moment, a heavy weight in the air, before Jack's voice broke the stillness.

"OK, we do it your way. But I would suggest one thing. If you find the passage branches off, mark the one you take somehow with a pile of rocks or a mark on the ground or something. That way, if you have to go back, then you can follow the path back or try a different one."

"Good idea," Sarah said, nodding her head in agreement.

"Alright, bro, take care of yourself, yeah?" Mirroring the latest trending social media handshake routine, Mason exchanged hand slaps with Jack, a grin on his face.

The sound of skin-on-skin contact made Sarah wince, but the cavern remained otherwise silent.

"Hey, you just worry about yourself. Don't break anything," Jack said.

He turned to Sarah. "Look after him for me. I don't need to tell you how awkward he is."

Sarah managed a smile. "I'll do my best, but he's a walking disaster. It's going to take all my effort just to make sure he doesn't hurt himself." She felt her tension ease a little at their banter. "Actually, you sure you don't want to take him?" she asked, exchanging knowing grins with Jack.

"Hey, come on!" Mason said, forgetting his volume.

"Shhhh!" Sarah and Jack hushed simultaneously before they burst into barely restrained giggles at Mason's chagrined expression.

"Alright, well, as fun as this pick on Mason session has been, should we get on with it?" he grumbled, his cheeks flushed from embarrassment.

"Sure thing, boss," Jack said, mocking Mason and his tendency to say the same, making Sarah stifle another laugh behind her hand.

"It's ok, sweety, I still love you," Sarah managed between muffled bouts of laughter. At this point, she wasn't even sure why she was laughing, but it sure felt good after what they'd all been through. *Laughter truly is medicine*, she thought to herself.

"Well, if you do, you're going to have to show me just how much," Mason said, regaining a semblance of his old self with a smirk and a wink directed at her.

"Ok, guys, this is it. What say we get ourselves some help and blow this joint?" Jack said, his voice brimming with renewed optimism and confidence.

His words hit Sarah like a cold bucket of water, sobering her instantly. Everything was riding on them finding a way out now. A queasy feeling began to form in the pit of her stomach as she looked between Mason and Jack, drinking in their ghostly and indistinct faces in the dim light to try to capture the moment in her mind. A cold dread snaked around her heart—this might very well be their last time together—and, unlike her previous doubts, she couldn't shake the icy grip of that thought.

The boys repeated their special handshake once again before giving each other a shoulder bump and parted, Jack swivelling back to face the narrow passage at the base of the wall.

"Come on, you," Sarah said, forcing herself into action. She grabbed Mason's arm and together, they walked toward the distant glow of the flashlight.

Was it her imagination, or was the glow a little duller than it had been when she left it?

Chapter Eighteen

In a far-off corner of the cavern, the large creature clung tightly to the biggest cluster of stalactites. It watched the three humans, for that is what it now remembered them as being, part with each other and head in separate directions. Its stomach rattled once more with hunger, as it switched its gaze between the two groups, contemplating which one to follow first. Its hunger said to take the one with the two humans, but its sense of self-preservation said it needed to take the safer option. Though, as ever with humans, they could be unpredictable. Many an encounter it had with them in the past had ended with unforeseen results. It had to be cautious. The sound of their laughter had triggered its fury and had almost caused it to make a mistake and attack early.

A mistake was something it couldn't afford. It watched the two humans head toward the passage that appeared to be the safer of the two. But it knew differently. Soon, they would find out what awaited them.

CHAPTER NINETEEN
ADAM

Adam sat up with a start, his heart pounding, as he blinked rapidly in the dim light. "You've got to be fucking kidding me," he muttered, as he jumped to his feet after checking his watch.

Somehow, he must have fallen asleep after Sarah and Mason had disappeared through the gap. A heavy silence had fallen over the trio after Mason and Sarah left. The silence was broken only by Adam asking both girls if they were alright and needed anything. The next thing he could recall, he had settled himself against the wall, trying to stay awake but obviously failing, given that an hour had passed, and he'd just woken up.

"What is it?" Christina groaned, turning her head to face him and blinking through the light at him.

"Oh shit, the light!" he muttered and looked in alarm at the flashlight still sitting upright and pointed at the cave roof. Its beam had significantly dimmed, to the point where he could only see the outline of the two girls' bodies now and not their faces.

"I must've fallen asleep. Fuck, I'm such an idiot," he said shaking his head.

"I must've too, you just woke me up," Christina said with another groan. She began to push herself up with her forearms, wincing with every movement.

"Hang on, let me help you," Adam said, walking over to her.

He grasped her under the arms, steadying her as he helped her sit up against the rough cave wall. Carefully, he slid Jack's jacket into place, pressing it against the jagged stone to offer a layer of padding. She leaned against it with a quiet sigh, the tension easing from her shoulders.

"How are you feeling? Any better?"

"A little," she admitted with a tired smile. "At least I'm not screaming anymore at the slightest movement, so that's a plus," she said.

Adam smiled and nodded before turning toward the dark shapeless form of Jenny, who had curled up against the opposite cave wall.

"Jenny? Are you awake?"

Silence was his answer, and there wasn't a hint of movement in response. He frowned, feeling unease wash over him, as he approached to kneel beside her. "Hey," he said softly. "Jenny?"

This far away from the dim light, she remained cloaked in darkness. After a soft shake with no response, he reached into his pocket for his phone. He yanked it out with a frantic tug, but the device slipped from his grasp, propelled by his haste. It hit the jagged ground with a sharp, resonant thud, the screen splintering into a mosaic of cracks.

"Oh god damn it!" he yelled in frustration.

He returned to grab the flashlight sitting in the middle of the trio and swung its faded light toward Jenny, who was lying on her side with her eyes closed. Her face was ghostly white and dripping with sweat. Tremors swept through her body sporadically as he placed the back of his hand on her forehead, feeling for her temperature. She felt red hot.

"Hey, Jenny?" he shook her softly, and to his relief, she began to stir.

"A... Adam?" she whispered, her eyes twitching as she fought to open them.

"I'm here," he said reassuringly, using his hand to wipe the sweat from her brow.

Her eyes fluttered a few more times before opening, and Adam struggled to contain a gasp.

The whites were a sickly yellow, clouded by a strange film, giving them a dull, lifeless appearance. The skin around them was raw and red, so irritated it looked as though it might bleed at any second.

"Adam, I... I don't feel good," she managed, her body shuddering with every word. "Water... I need... Water," she whispered, her mouth parting to lick her parched lips. Her tongue was almost the same angry, inflamed red shade as the skin ringing her eyes.

"OK, hang on, my backpack is... oh shit," he said, his stomach sinking when he realized that the backpacks were still at the cave entrance. Sarah and Mason were meant to bring them back with them, but had obviously forgotten.

"I'll go get you some, just hang in there, ok?" he said, his mind and heart racing as he swept back a strand of hair that had begun to creep over her eyes from her trembling.

"OK..." she whispered, then closed her eyes once more.

Adam berated himself for his carelessness. He should have noticed that Sarah and Mason had returned without their backpacks. He was supposed to look after the two girls, and he couldn't even do something as simple as making sure they had water. Rising to his feet, he retrieved his phone from the ground and tapped on the spider-webbed screen, hoping for some response. Nothing. It was dead. Sighing, he slipped it back into his pocket and returned to Christina.

"Hey, I'm going to head back to the entrance to grab our backpacks and sleeping bags," he said, pausing to look back over his shoulder to the shivering outline of Jenny.

"She's not doing so well, huh?" Christina said softly, following his gaze toward Jenny.

Adam turned to face Christina, his shoulders slumped, and shook his head dejectedly, a sigh escaping his lips. "No, she's not. We can only hope Sarah, Mason, and Jack can find a way to get help quickly."

Christina nodded, shuffling to reposition herself.

"Hey, so I kinda smashed my phone when I dropped it, so I'm going to need to take the flashlight. Do you still have yours with you?"

"No, I think I dropped it somewhere in the chaos of the attack," she said glumly.

"Oh yeah, of course. Do you have your phone with you? Are you able to use that?"

Christina patted her jean pocket and nodded before pulling it out and tapping on the screen to turn the flash-light on.

"OK, I'll be back as soon as I can," Adam said as he turned toward the corridor leading to the cave entrance.

"Don't break your back carrying everything," Christina said from behind him.

"Hey, if I can carry a backpack, a sleeping bag, and two twenty-four cases of beer up a mountain, I can handle it," he threw back over his shoulder.

Anxiety coiled in Adam's gut as he headed back toward

the entrance, a relentless, creeping dread. Jenny was in more trouble than he'd thought. He feared to think what might happen if the trio searching for a way out didn't find one soon.

Chapter Twenty
Sarah

Mason stopped behind Sarah, shining his flashlight on her as she bent over to pick up her own. Her short skirt rode upwards, exposing a hint of her panties and toned ass and he grinned in appreciation. Despite himself, he was starting to feel horny. Maybe if they were lucky enough and found another cavern ahead, he could get himself a piece of that. He felt himself beginning to harden at the thought, and he forced himself to concentrate on the task at hand. Still, he couldn't deny this whole thing was exciting. Here they were in a cave system that no one knew about, searching for a way out on a rescue mission to save their friends. It was almost as if he were starring in an adventure movie. Sure, if they didn't find help, they were pretty much fucked, but he had to focus on something to keep him going. That something was right in front of him.

Sarah turned around with flashlight in hand, capturing the direction of his eyes just before they drifted back up to meet hers.

"Were you just staring at my ass?" she asked, a hint of disgust mixed with amusement in the smirk she gave him.

"Well, I mean, there's not much else in here to stare at," he said lamely with a wide smile.

"You're here in a cave beneath the Adirondack mountains, filled with natural beauty, and you think there's nothing else to stare at but my ass?"

"Your ass IS a natural beauty," he quipped, his grin expanding ever wider.

"You're hopeless," Sarah sighed, shaking her head with a smile of her own. "C'mon then, you can stare at my ass while I search for a way out," she said, putting the emphasis on the I.

"Sounds good to me," he said, his eyes already drifting in that direction.

She laughed, turned, and headed into the passage before them, adding an extra sway to her hips with each step, much to Mason's delight.

She frowned at the yellowish tint of the torchlight aimed before her. There was no doubt it had dimmed, which emphasised the importance of their mission. Luckily, they still had Mason's flashlight and their phones for backup if worse came to worst.

The air grew cooler as they ventured deeper, a gentle breeze whispering through the darkness, carrying with it the promise of something unknown. Despite the non-appearance of the thing that had caused the shriek Jack had mentioned, it didn't diminish the unsettling feeling she had, and she moved cautiously, each step measured and deliberate. Her soft footsteps contrasted sharply with Mason's heavy, awkward ones, making her efforts seem pointless.

The passage meandered a little, heading deeper into the mountain, its consistent height offering a much easier journey than the one Jack was no doubt having to endure. She allowed her mind to drift a little, exploring the possibilities of where the passage might take them. If they weren't in such a dire situation, she would have loved to explore the cave system, but time was short. She could only hope this passage would be the one to lead them out.

Their path was taking them in an upward direction as the breeze grew stronger. Sarah's hopes began to rise. It had been somewhere in the vicinity of ten minutes since they had first entered the passage, and they had travelled some distance. Could it be the exit lay ahead of them? A faint, ethereal glow appeared, and she quickened her pace as the passage gradually widened until she reached its exit.

Emerging into a vast, open cavern, Sarah gasped at the sight before her.

"OK, now it's not just your ass I'm admiring," she heard Mason say behind her along with an intake of breath.

The ceiling soared high above them, furnished with clusters of radiant green moss that bathed the entire space in a soft, otherworldly light. At the center of the cavern lay a large, serene pool of water, almost lake-like in size, its surface shimmering with the reflections of the glowing moss. A few sizeable boulders sat near the edge of the pool, a quick scan of the ceiling above revealing their origin. A cool breeze rippled across the water, creating gentle waves that lapped at the rocky shore.

Sarah marvelled at the sight. It felt as though she had stumbled upon a hidden sanctuary, untouched by time. Searching for the source of the breeze, she saw a portion of the far cave wall honeycombed by fist-sized holes. The breeze was carried from them across the water and toward the passage they had emerged from. She felt her spirits dampen until she spotted another opening to a passage on the other side of the lapping water. The path to it was narrow, but they should be able to shimmy along the gap between the cave wall and the pool of water to get to it.

She turned her attention back to the water, switched off the flashlight, and took in the magnificence of what lay before them once more. Somehow, there was something romantic about the scene. Nature's splendour lay ahead of them, something that no one else had laid their eyes on, and it was undeniably beautiful. Mason's arms wrapped around her waist from behind, and the pair stood still, awed by their surroundings.

A few moments later, the serenity was broken by Mason shuffling behind her as his hands began to wander northwards. A jolt of excitement shot through Sarah at his touch; his fingertips sent shivers of electricity across her skin.

Expertly sliding up over her smooth stomach, his hands slipped underneath her crop top with practiced ease and cupped her breasts, kneading them firmly. She groaned as he played with her, feeling him harden against her rump as his hands pulled down her bra. His fingers sought and found her nipples as he pulled her against him. She pushed herself back into his straining jeans, enjoying the feel of his bulge against her ass as she began to grind against him, evoking more groans of desire in her ear.

Spinning around, she pulled his head towards hers, giving him a gentle, teasing nip on his lips and pulling away, her mouth inches away from his, enjoying his desperate panting breaths and efforts to place his lips on hers. As his breathing became more ragged, she gave in and kissed him slowly and passionately, a sensual exploration of tongues as he moaned in need.

Pulling away, she grabbed his hand and moved toward one of the boulders near the shoreline, swaying her hips as she did so, letting out a small gasp as Mason's hand slapped playfully on her ass.

Reaching the boulder, she spun around and removed

her crop top, exposing the delicate lace of her perfectly fitted and filled Victoria's Secret bra.

Mason watched, his eyes ablaze with desire, as she shimmied her short skirt down her legs. Her almost see-through lace panties revealed beneath were a perfect match to her bra and barely hid her womanhood.

Standing back up slowly, she felt the weight of his gaze linger on her cleavage before they rose to finally, deliberately, meet her eyes. Reaching behind her back, she unpinned her bra, letting the straps fall over her shoulders as she held it in her hands, covering her generous breasts. He began to step forward, but she shifted, one hand holding her bra in place, the other hand waving a finger held high in a playful refusal.

He groaned once more but stepped back and continued to watch.

Sarah smiled at him in the way she knew drove him mad and removed her arm, letting the bra fall to the ground, exposing her perfect and pert tits for his eyes to feast on. Feast on them they did, as she began to cup them in her hands, extending a finger on each to play with her nipples, making them harden.

She watched Mason shift and groan anxiously, his hands rubbing his crotch, enjoying the feeling of power she had over him.

"I think you're wearing too much clothing, mister," she purred.

She laughed as his hands, shaking with need, fumbled with his belt to undo it, pulling them down over his boxers. His hands flew to his shirt and lifted it off, and Sarah bit her lip as she saw his bulging pecs and rippling abs, the dim lighting in the cavern placing shadows in all the right places on his body.

Before he could reach for his boxers, she extended a finger and bent it toward her in a come-hither gesture.

His desire was so great, he almost ran toward her, bringing another smile to Sarah's lips. Just before he reached her, she held up her hand for him to stop and stepped forward, extending her hands and running them down his toned chest and arms, enjoying the feel of each muscle as her hands explored his taut body.

Tracing a path down his abs and over the waistband of his boxers, she hesitated there for a moment as she drank in his desire once more before sliding her hand over the bulge in the front.

She moaned softly, grabbing one of his hands and placing it on her breast, his other hand joining in and kneading the other. She felt him shift beneath her strokes as she rubbed him through his boxers, and after a few moments, she stepped back once more.

Reaching for her panties, she slid them down, feeling the wetness between her legs, her desire reaching a fever pitch. Standing up, she pointed at his boxers, prompting him to hastily pull them down, revealing his 7-inch erect cock already dripping in anticipation.

Without a word, she turned around and bent over, leaning against the boulder, opening herself up for Mason's erect manhood to enter her moist sex.

She didn't have to wait long. She felt Mason grip onto her waist as he slid his cock into her hole, the pair moaning in plea-sure as he filled her until his balls made contact with her ass. The excitement she felt was unlike any she'd experienced before. They were deep within a mountain, in a cave filled with natural beauty, and the urgency of their situation made things seem forbidden. It felt wrong, and she knew that it was, but there was no denying the rush she was feeling. Mason began to thrust in and out of her, just the way she liked it, and she leant over further to give him more room. He took advantage of it and gripped onto her waist, pounding his hard cock deep into her. The cave was filled with their pleasure, their voices mixing together in an erotic choir, building up to a crescendo.

Mason leaned forward and reached for her breasts, cupping them in his hands as he rammed into her. She felt him building to a climax, and that knowledge made hers build too. With a few more final thrusts, he released into her, and she felt his seed fill her, just as she climaxed herself. Together, their voices were as one, as their fulfilled cries echoed in the cavernous space.

Panting heavily, Sarah turned around and leant back on the boulder, her legs quivering from the release of pleasure.

"Man, I've been wanting to do that ever since we got into the cave," Mason said, grinning widely, his eyes still roaming and admiring her body.

"Would have been a little embarrassing in front of the others. I'm no exhibitionist, you know," she joked, smiling back at him.

She was just about to pick up her discarded clothes when the water caught her eye. "I'm going to jump in the water for a minute and wash off; it feels like you poured a gallon of your man juice into me this time. Just a little excited, were we?" she said with a mischievous grin.

"Wait, what? You're going in there? What if there's something in there?"

"What, like a shark?" Sarah chuckled. "Oh, Mason, you worry too much sometimes," she said, shaking her head, but still smiling.

She rounded the boulder and approached the water's edge. It really was beautiful here. Humans had wrecked so much natural beauty of the world, but here, it remained unspoiled. Until now, that is. But a quick dip in the water to wash off was hardly going to ruin anything.

She dipped a toe into the lake and recoiled with a shiver. Although she expected the water to be cold, its icy chill still shocked her.

Defying her natural instincts, she took a deep breath and entered the water, gasping in shock with each step as the freezing water hit her warm skin. Ripples spread from every footstep, disturbing the otherwise perfect stillness of the water's surface. The rocks under her feet felt slimy and algae-covered, but she kept on regardless, gritting her teeth. When she was up to her waist, she decided to just dive in and get the torture of the cold water hitting each body part over with in one go.

With another deep breath to prepare herself, she raised her arms over her head and launched herself into the pristine pool.

The frigid water enveloped her, sending a jolt of shock through her body as she sank beneath the surface. The cold was beyond anything she had ever experienced before, a piercing, bone-chilling sensation that seemed to freeze her from the inside out. Her muscles seized up, and for a terrifying second, she couldn't move. The water felt like a thousand needles pricking her skin, each one sharper and more relentless than the last.

Sarah's heart pounded wildly, each beat echoing in her ears like a drum. Instinctively, she kicked her legs and flailed her arms, desperate to break the surface and escape the numbing cold.

As she emerged, gasping for breath, the shock began to subside, replaced by a dull, throbbing ache that spread through her limbs. The cold still clung to her, but she could feel her body slowly adjusting, the initial shock giving way to a strange, exhilarating clarity. Every nerve was electrified, every sense heightened, and for a moment, she felt more alive than she ever had before.

Then she became aware of Mason's shriek. Wiping her eyes free of water, she looked toward the shore. Mason, now fully clothed, was jumping up and down and screaming, his finger pointed towards her, his voice incomprehensible and dulled by the water in her ears.

"I'm ok," she called out, confused by his reaction. She hadn't been under the water that long, had she?

Mason began to wade into the water, still screaming, and then his words began to dawn on her.

"Behind you!" he shouted, his voice raw with terror, the sound echoing through the cavern.

Sarah turned around, puzzled, and then froze in shock at the sight before her.

Large, luminous eyes met hers, and she blinked slowly, trying to get a grasp on what she was seeing.

The eyes, cold and reptilian, belonged to a large snake-like head, attached to a long, sinuous body that seemed to writhe even when still beneath the rippling water's surface. As panicked as she now was, she could see the thing was big, at least six feet long. Its head was ridged, the surface covered in dark hardened silvery skin blanketed in bumps. Its teeth were exposed, sharp and jagged, lining its powerful-looking jaws. Its neck bore a distinctive red band, a stark contrast to its otherwise silvery form. A strange, white, almost star-shaped pattern on its forehead completed the terrifying picture. It was as if a myth had come to life right before her eyes and its own, filled with hunger, were set firmly on her.

She screamed and began to wave her arms wildly, trying to propel herself backward, her legs churning the water, finding no solid ground beneath them. She must've dived in too far, or the bottom of the pool was unreachable where she was.

"Hey, you big giant piece of shit, leave her alone! Yeah, that's right, you fuckin' oversized sea snake, I'm talking to you!" Mason screamed before his flashlight arced over Sarah's head and smacked into the creature's snout.

The beast didn't react. Instead, it extended its head higher over Sarah, as she continued to scream in raw terror, desperately paddling herself backwards, unwilling to turn around to take her eyes off the threat before her.

With a ragged, gurgling hiss, its head plunged down toward Sarah at lightning speed. She barely had time to feel pain before the creature's jaws clamped down, its razor-sharp teeth tearing into her waist with a sickening crunch, and her body exploded in a bloody spray as it cleaved her in two.

Chapter Twenty-One
Christina

Christina's eyes snapped open to a disorienting fog clouding her mind. It took her a few moments to realize she'd fallen asleep again, only minutes after Adam had left to get the backpacks. A quick check of her phone revealed the time was now 11:45 pm, almost thirty minutes since Adam had left. Surely he should have been back by now. A faint unease crept into her chest. She squirmed, trying to find a more comfortable position, but to no avail. Her back was still burning, but the pain had lessened somewhat. It was still enough to elicit a wince with each movement.

She reached for the first aid kit nearby and opened it, grabbing the nearly empty painkiller bottle. She opened it and took out a couple, dry swallowing them, hoping they would kick in soon.

Her numb backside felt like it was fused to the cold, rough surface of the cave ground. The thought of eventually standing brought a fresh wave of dread. The attempt, she knew, would bring agonizing pain.

She decided she would wait for Adam to return and

the meds to kick in before testing it out. She couldn't sit here until rescue came. That is, if it came at all. A fresh pang of worry hit her at the thought. She knew if anyone could find help, it would be Jack and Mason. The fact that Sarah was there too to help focus them and keep them on track only helped their chances. She just had to trust in them.

She sighed and shifted position again, feeling restless.

Suddenly, a loud, harsh, laboured gasp rang out from the opposite side of the cave where Jenny's darkened form lay.

"Jenny? Are you OK?" Christina called out.

Rasping, uneven panting following the gasp was her only answer.

Christina felt a surge of fear and concern, her heartbeat quickening in her chest. Where the fuck was Adam? It sounded like Jenny was having some sort of seizure.

Christina extended her arm toward Jenny, aiming her phone's flashlight at her, but the light didn't reveal much besides Jenny's curled-up, quivering form. Suddenly, spasms began to wrack Jenny's body as a continued symphony of suffering poured from her, punctuated by strange guttural noises that sent chills down Christina's spine.

"Goddamn it Adam, if you're close, hurry the fuck up! Jenny's having a seizure," Christina screamed.

A small cry of pain erupted from Christina's lips as she strained against the tight bandages around her midriff and back, eventually succeeding in getting onto her hands and knees.

"Hang on, Jenny, I'm coming," she said as she reached for the phone next to her.

"Jenny? Holy shit, hang on," Adam's panicked voice echoed from the direction of the corridor. The dull thud of the backpacks and sleeping bags he had been carrying hit the floor as he came into view, racing toward Jenny.

"About fucking time," Christina called out with a pained groan. She pushed herself up, her muscles protesting with every inch of movement. Her arms trembled under the strain and the pain, but she gritted her teeth and forced herself to continue. As she finally managed to sit back on her heels, Christina paused to catch her breath and wait for the stars in her eyes to fade. Once they did, she directed her gaze toward the chaotic movements of Adam and Jenny.

Adam had his hands placed on Jenny's shoulders, struggling to hold her in position to protect her head as she thrashed and jerked. The strange guttural noises she had been making now sounded more animalistic somehow, turning into grunting and a high-pitched, almost inhuman growl. Sharp cracking sounds, like bone snapping or readjusting into new positions, punctuated her unnatural cries. Each snap echoed and bounced off the cave walls, amplifying the horrifying sound. A series of sickening pops filled the air, making Christina's stomach roil as an icy spike of fear shot down her spine.

"Adam what the fuck is happening?" she screamed.

From her position, she could only see Adam's back and Jenny's wildly gyrating waist and legs.

"I... I don't know. It looks like... No... what the fuck?!" His voice rose in a crescendo of shock. In the blink of an eye, Christina saw him fall backwards onto his ass as he began to back pedal in panicked movements.

Christina gasped in shock as Jenny rose to her feet with a sharp, unnatural movement. Adam shone his flashlight on her as he scrambled to his feet and froze in place. Jenny's head hung low, and she began to twist and gyrate in place. The same animalistic sounds she had been making before seemed clearer and more pronounced. Her body jerked and flinched as the sickening snapping and popping sounds continued. It wasn't long before the purpose of the sounds became clear.

Her body expanded outward, bulging and reshaping itself. The unnatural chorus swelled with the sound of tearing fabric as two monstrous, triangular shapes sprouted from Jenny's back, blossoming into fleshy wings. Her arms thinned and stretched out, her fingernails expanding outwards into sharp, curved talons. With a sharp crack, she arched her spine, her posture becoming grotesquely hunched; her skull elongated and narrowed, taking on an undeniable batlike appearance. The soft skin of her face hardened as the muscle and bone beneath shifted, twisting into a grotesque parody of humanity before transforming into something rough, pitted, and sharply curved. Her eyes lost their brown color as they sank deep within their sockets and began to glow with an unnatural, sickly yellow light. Her nose split in two with a sharp crack, and a hardened, ridged bone grew in between, the nostrils extending upwards and twitching as if adjusting to its new form. Beneath her torn clothes, her skin was so pale it was almost transparent, revealing a frightening array of dark, pulsing veins in the glow of the flashlight.

The creature before them, once Jenny, trembled violently, a testament to the trauma of its transformation. Frozen in shock, Christina and Adam stared at the thing in horror. Hot tears welled in Christina's eyes, blurring her vision. Her friend, with whom she had grown so close lately, was now gone. The pain Jenny must have gone through in the transformation would have been immense, her suffering immeasurable, and now what remained of her had turned into something impossible. Something that shouldn't be able to exist anywhere outside of a movie.

Christina hauled herself to her feet, ignoring the pangs

of pain shooting down her back, trying to contain the sobs that threatened to wrack her body.

"Jenny? Honey, can you hear me? It's me, Christina. Are you still there? Please tell me you're still there." Tears spilled down her cheeks, but the creature remained still, its trembling slowly losing its intensity.

"Oh god, Jenny, no," Adam managed, his own legs quivering as he staggered backwards.

The sudden movement caught the creature's eye, and it raised its head to stare at Adam, its features transforming into animalistic hunger and rage. Without a warning, it launched itself at him with an ear-splitting shriek, talons extended. Its claws tore through his clothing and embedded themselves into the flesh beneath, sending plumes of blood into the air. Driven backward by the weight of the creature, Adam fell with a heavy thud onto the ground. His head collided with the rocks beneath with a sickening crack as the flashlight flew from his hands, clattering to a stop near Christina's feet.

"Jenny, no!" With a final, desperate scream, Christina tried to reach the Jenny hidden within the monstrous transformation.

Ignoring her, the creature straddled Adam's chest, staring at his face with cold fascination as his mouth gaped open and closed, a gruesome stream of blood bubbling and pouring out from the corners. It cocked its head as it continued to watch him, a fleeting expression of recognition and horror crossing its face before it gave way to a look of undeniable hunger.

It tore its talons from Adam's chest, his body lurching upwards before thudding back onto the unforgiving rock floor, his head cracking against the stone with a nauseating crunch. A wet, choking gurgle tore itself from Adam's throat as the monstrous creature loomed over him. His eyes mercifully rolled back just before the creature plunged its head down and sank its needle-sharp teeth into his neck and tore out a chunk of flesh, sending a shower of blood onto the cave walls.

A scream caught in Christina's throat, her stomach roiling as the creature chewed the piece methodically and watched Adam's life drain away. Its nose twitched as it took in the metallic scent of blood from the body beneath.

Christina began to inch herself toward Adam's abandoned flashlight, crouching down slowly to pick it up. Her eyes remained trained on the monster, trying to make sure she didn't make any sudden movements.

She took a deep breath when her trembling hand touched the flashlight and froze, as the creature stiffened after swallowing the chunk of bloody meat, its body shuddering briefly as if it were adjusting to its new diet.

After a few more moments, it thrust its head back down towards Adam's ruined throat and began to rip and tear. It slurped at the crimson liquid spilling from his wounds and gulped down pieces of meat in a display that turned Christina's stomach to mush. She picked up the flashlight, only just able to turn her head at the last moment to vomit onto the ground, wincing at the sound of the splash hitting the rock. The creature's nose twitched, but its attention was still completely on its meal.

Christina took the opportunity to creep toward the gap in the cave wall. Easing herself in, she winced with each movement and rock that poked into her already damaged back, but her path this time was easier. Learning from her mistakes, she ducked beneath the outcropping of rock that she had gotten caught on initially and kept going. Behind her, the sound of feeding continued, and Christina had to take deep breaths to try to calm her turbulent stomach.

The journey through seemed to take an age. Her heart

felt like a frantic bird trapped in her chest, her head reeling from the terrifying images and the fear that the creature would be after her at any moment.

With one final shimmy, she was through and out into the ominous expanse of the never-ending darkness.

Throwing a look back over her shoulder at the gap, she stumbled forward, moving as fast as her body would allow. She had to locate the others and find a way out of this deathtrap of a cave system before whatever the fuck Jenny had turned into made them all its next meal.

Chapter Twenty-Two
Jack

Jack slid his backpack off his shoulders and shoved it into the tunnel in front of him. He crouched down to shine his flashlight inside and looked around the small space, mentally preparing for his journey. He could hear Sarah's laughter as she and Mason headed to the opposite side of the cave toward their passage. It seemed as if his warning about whatever made the shriek had been forgotten, but to be fair, there had been no further sign of it. He could almost convince himself he had imagined it if not for the vividly recalled nightmarish sound that continued to haunt the hallways of his mind. Still, he felt more at ease as time passed. Perhaps it had just been some startled cave resident that had been freaked out by hearing an unfamiliar sound in its domain.

He shrugged the thought off and began to crawl inside the tunnel. Lucky for him, on hands and knees, he still had room to spare above him, so the danger of getting stuck was non-existent, at least for now. The air began to thicken with the moist heat of whatever lay ahead. A wave of sulfurous stench, like a thousand rotten eggs, hit him, making him gag, but he found himself getting used to it as he continued.

The tunnel began to slope upwards as it twisted and turned, and soon Jack lost track of which direction he had first come from and where the tunnel was heading. Sweat began to pour off his body, his heart pounding from exertion and the effort to drag enough oxygen from the cloying heat into his lungs. His body cried out for water, but he pressed on, determined to reach an exit before he gave in to his urge. The constant scraping of his elbows and knees against the rough stone began to cause a stinging pain. No doubt, he would be left with a few cuts and bruises to join the others he had from navigating through the tight gap. As he rounded another bend in the tunnel, he could see a faint, eerie reddish glow illuminating the path ahead.

As Jack moved closer, waves of heat rolled toward him as the glow intensified, casting flickering shadows on the tunnel walls. Another bend appeared before him, and it looked like the source of the light and heat was just around the corner. Jack felt his anticipation building, mixed with a tinge of apprehension.

Rounding the corner, he gasped in relief as he saw it open out to another passage, the reddish glow more apparent on the cave wall on the opposite side. The incandescence seemed to originate from the left of the exit. He scrambled the last few feet, pushing the backpack in front of him into the passage, and crawled out, rising with a wince to his feet, feeling his raw knees scream in protest.

He turned toward the left and scanned the area before him with his flashlight. The tunnel he was standing in was high but narrow, allowing only enough room for one person to traverse at a time. The scarlet light intensified over the length of the foreseeable tunnel. Turning to the right, he examined the path in that direction, finding only more darkness beyond the reach of his flashlight's beam.

His curiosity temporarily satisfied, Jack searched through his backpack for a bottle of water and uncapped it. He paused for a moment, stuck in a tug of war between his common sense telling him not to take in too much and his body screaming at him to drink the whole thing. He settled for a middle ground, ignoring the warnings in his mind about conserving it, and drank about half the bottle in one gulp. Capping the bottle once more, he wiped his lips with the back of his hand and shoved the bottle back into his backpack.

Deciding to check out the direction of the strange glow first, he picked up his backpack and threw it over his shoulders, making sure it was secure. There was enough light to navigate without the flashlight ahead, so he switched it off. He had to conserve batteries now, especially since his phone's was low and he didn't want to resort to using its battery-draining flashlight functionality if he could avoid it.

He rounded the corner and stopped, his eyes widening in disbelief. Ahead of him, the tunnel expanded out into a small cavern, every inch of the ground covered by a thermal spring. Its dense water was a muddy red color, as if the earth itself had bled into the pool. Its surface bubbled and churned, occasionally sending small splashes onto the cave walls, which had begun to smooth out from the intense heat of the water. Steam rose in thick, swirling tendrils, carrying with it the scent of minerals and iron, which combined to create the rotten egg smell he had detected in the tunnel. A few small rents in the cavern's roof attracted the steam and took it on a journey, its destination a secret only the cave could tell.

Jack advanced toward the pool as close as the heat would allow, marvelling at the sight. The Adirondack

Mountains were not known for such phenomena, making this discovery all the more extraordinary. The only place he knew of with thermal springs was the Saratoga Springs area, located quite a distance east of where they were. This night was definitely a night for firsts, that was for sure.

He retreated down the tunnel away from the stifling heat, setting down his backpack and rifling through it to retrieve the half-full bottle of water. This time, as he stared at it, his common sense prevailed, and he decided to preserve it. After all, who knew how far the way out would be, if there was even one in this part of the cave system?

Jack threw the backpack over his shoulder again and switched on his flashlight, directing it towards the darkness of the passage opposite the thermal spring. He followed it only to find it ended in a small cavern with three branching passages.

A frustrated "Shit" escaped his lips as he spun in the cavern's center. His flashlight beam sliced through the oppressive darkness, desperately seeking a hint, a sign, any clue that one of the narrow passages might lead him to the surface. Every one of them looked the same. He would have to take a guess.

His mind raced, trying to work out what to do when his eyes fell on some stones scattered around the base of the cavern wall. He recalled his plan to leave behind an indication of which path he would take and grinned. Sometimes, even he was impressed with his genius. If by chance the passage he took did lead out, it would tell anyone following him which direction to go. Now he just had to choose one.

He swept his flashlight across the passages again, searching for some overlooked clue that would guide him as to which one to try first, but much to his frustration, found nothing. He decided the most logical choice was to take the left passage and work his way through them to the right if it didn't lead anywhere. Gathering the stones he needed, he formed them into a crude arrow shape pointing to the left passage. He stood back up and brushed his hands off on his already dirty jeans before heading into the chosen passage, his footsteps echoing softly against the craggy walls.

The tunnel twisted and turned, eventually branching into two more passages. He hesitated for a moment, then decided to follow the one on the right. He gathered more discarded rocks, fashioned an arrow, and headed down the passage.

As he continued, the tunnel seemed to loop and wind in a disorienting maze of cold, damp stone, and Jack's sense of direction wavered. Suddenly, he emerged into a familiar cavern—the same one he had originally found with the three passages, and he had exited from the one on the right. He had come full circle. Only when he looked for the arrow he had made, he couldn't find it.

"What the fuck?"

He spun around, a deep frown furrowing his brow as he scanned the cavern floor, searching for any sign of tampering. The rocks he had placed had vanished as if they never existed. Aside from the bare patches where he'd gathered them, there was no evidence that he'd ever been there. Was he in a different section of the cave or something? That had to be the only possible answer; there was no one else in here with him.

"Fuck this," Jack muttered, feeling slightly spooked by the situation. He gathered up more rocks, this time pointing them towards the center passage, entering it when done.

Similar to the other passage he had taken, this one also meandered and twisted around, but then began to narrow until it reached a dead end. Sighing in frustration, he was about to turn back when something caught his eye—a small hole in the center of the dead-end wall, just big enough to peer through.

Curiosity got the better of him, and he crouched down, pressing his eye to the hole. At first, he saw nothing but darkness. But then, he felt a sudden gust of wind directed toward his eye as the darkness seemed to shift across his field of vision. Jack fell back on his ass, his breath caught in his throat and then suddenly, he heard it—a deep, rhythmic pounding, like the sound of heavy stomping echoing through a cavern from the other side. The ground beneath him seemed to tremble with each thud, his heart pounding in time with the mysterious footsteps.

"What the... What the fuck was that?" Jack whispered, his voice quivering with fear as they faded into the distance.

Scrambling to his feet, he wasted little time in retreating the way he came, half expecting whatever had made those footsteps to burst through the wall behind him and pursue.

His heart sank when he arrived back at the cavern. The rock pile he had shaped into an arrow had been scattered across the floor as if something or someone had kicked it.

"You fucking asshole," he screamed, flinching as the cave magnified his shout. "I'm going to fucking kill you if I find you. It better not be you, Mason, you prick."

A torrent of anger, hot and furious, coursed through him. It was obvious someone was playing a prank on him. Grabbing his backpack, he searched for his water bottle, uncapped it, and took a long swallow. His mind was so focused on who it could be that he didn't realise what he was doing until he pulled the bottle from his lips and saw there was only a mouthful of water left.

"Oh, goddamn it, that's just perfect," he said, his anger fuelled even further by his absentminded waste of precious water.

He took some deep breaths, trying to compose himself

until he finally felt calm enough to decide his next move. There was only one tunnel that led to another branching passage, and that was the left one.

He shone his flashlight onto the scattered rocks and sighed heavily, gathering them once more to create an arrow pointing left. His anger began to simmer again, a low, burning heat spreading through his chest. Hopefully, the last passage open to him at the branch ahead would take him to the other side of the dead end, where he had heard the prankster. Whoever it was would be dead meat. Dusting himself off once more, he stood up, threw his backpack over his shoulder, and headed into the tunnel.

Chapter Twenty-Three

Amusement filled the creature, a feeling it had not felt for an untold amount of time. Having followed the large lone human via a gap high up in the cavern where no human flashlight could reach, it had been watching, biding its time.

Its hunger was undeniable, but this time its will was stronger. It knew its body well enough to know just how long it could push it before it had to take action. Having a food source so nearby and now separated from the pack meant that it could enjoy the hunt. And enjoy it, it had.

The large human was clumsy, loud, and easy to follow, and the creature knew every inch of the tunnel system the human had unwittingly entered. Removing the rocks the human used as a tracking system was simple, and seeing the human give in to its emotions was more than worth the payoff. The meat was tastier when they were stimulated.

There was something about these humans, something that made it angry. Something from long ago, but when it tried to think about it, it slipped through its mind like sand. All it knew was that these creatures needed to suffer, the same way it had suffered from something done to it long ago. The thought of draining every last bit of hope from these beings, leaving them whimpering and broken, was almost as delightful as the anticipated feast of blood and flesh that would follow.

CHAPTER TWENTY-FOUR
MASON

"Sarah, noooooooo!" Mason screamed as he watched Sarah's lower half sink beneath the roiling water. As soon as the creature had cleaved her in two with its razor-sharp teeth, it dove back under the water with Sarah's upper body trapped within its jaws, leaving a trail of bloody crimson in its wake.

Unable to think, only feeling the weight of his grief for Sarah, Mason flung himself into the water after the monster, the cold a momentary distraction from his pain. Following the crimson blood trail that snaked downward and toward the back of the cave, Mason propelled himself through the water in desperation. The vision of her death replayed over and over in his mind. His body was wracked with panic, fear, anger, and sorrow, and he couldn't help but think that this was his fault somehow. That if he hadn't thought about himself and his own desires, she would still be alive. He knew logically that Sarah was gone, and his pursuit was pointless, yet the blood trail pulled him forward, his common sense clouded by grief and an irrational hope.

The trail took a sudden dive toward the bottom. He hesitated, his lungs burning, his body screaming for air, before he thrashed toward the surface, gasping for breath and sucking it in before diving down once more. The blood trail had begun to thin, but was still thick enough to follow. The deeper he went, the darker it got, the luminescent glow from the cavern not strong enough to penetrate the depths he was headed into. Before him, a gaping blackness yawned open, the blood trail disappearing into its depths. He swam toward it, searching desperately for any sign of light so that he could continue. His body began to beg for air once more; he had to resurface. He was on the verge of turning to head back when a subtle movement in the darkness caught his attention; something was floating there. He pushed aside his body's instinct to surface and swam closer for a better look. It was Sarah's severed arm, the pale fleshy fibres of muscle tissue swaying gently in the water. His world shattered as reality hit him with the force of a truck, and he gave in to his body's need for air, his arms and legs working on autopilot as he rose to the surface.

He made his way back to the shore on shaky legs. His tears joined Sarah's blood in the previously pristine water, once bound together by life and now by death.

Reaching the edge of the shoreline, he lay on his back, his feet dangling in the water, uncaring if the creature came back. His chest heaved, a ragged, painful rhythm accompanying the silent scream of his grief. The thought of never seeing Sarah again was a physical blow, a gut-wrenching pain that stole the air from his lungs.

He and Sarah had been an item since freshman year. They had become inseparable since then, their personalities, their zest for life, their similar carefree attitudes, and caring qualities they kept hidden behind who they portrayed themselves as, all fitting together perfectly. Now she was gone, and it felt like part of him had been irretrievably lost, that he would never be whole again. He continued to lie there sobbing, half of him hoping the creature would come back and end his suffering. Memories came crashing back into his mind like a movie, every scene heartbreaking. Her smile, her laugh, her voice, her seductive teasing, every recollection hitting him in the stomach like a punch. Even as grief continued to fill him and his eyes continued to leak tears, he felt an overwhelming weariness flood through him, and he found himself fighting to hold his eyes open, eventually succumbing to the temporary respite of sleep.

Chapter Twenty-Five
Jack

Jack trudged onward through the tunnel wearily. After reaching the branching passage, he had taken the left one. He hadn't been surprised to see the stones he had arranged to point at the right passage scattered once more, but he had still known which direction to take.

It had seemed like hours since then. The unwavering straight line the tunnel took him on, combined with the unchanging landscape, began to eat at him. He could feel the exhaustion seeping into his bones, a leaden weight in his limbs from exertion and the night's events. He glanced at the greenish tinge of the watch face on his wrist. It was almost 2:00 am.

He thought briefly about finding somewhere to rest, but then thoughts of Jenny and especially Christina filled him with guilt. He had to keep going; the others were relying on him. His phone was dead, so calling for help or sending a message was no longer an option. His hopes were now pinned entirely on the tunnel he was following. If it didn't lead anywhere, then hopefully Mason's and Sarah's passage did.

The cave unexpectedly opened up before him, pulling his attention away from his thoughts. Quickening his pace, trying to keep his rising hope at bay, he exited the tunnel into a small cavern.

The air was cooler here, and the sound of dripping water filled the space. In the center of the cavern, a small pool of water shimmered in the glow of his torchlight, fed by a gentle trickle running down the fluorescent moss-covered walls. The sight of another passage on the other side filled him with relief; there was still a way forward.

There was enough light to see without his flashlight, so he switched it off and approached the pool, kneeling beside it to take a closer look. The water was clear and inviting, a stark contrast to the rugged surroundings. The pool was close to overflowing and spilling onto the floor, but never did. He guessed there must be some sort of chute at the bottom to carry the water to another area within the cave system.

Jack noticed a faint breeze stirring the air, bringing with it a hint of freshness. He looked up and saw its source—a small dark hole in the roof of the cave.

His thoughts turned to the possibilities of what lay above. Was the exit right over him? Was he close to the surface? He switched on his flashlight once more and directed its beam through the small hole and sighed in disappointment when he saw only the craggy surface of the ceiling beyond. Still, the cool air had to be coming from somewhere, and it felt like a good sign.

He switched off the flashlight and turned his attention back to the small pool. Since his water was running low, he decided to chance a mouthful to test it before he filled his bottle.

He cupped his hands and scooped up some of the clear water. The cool liquid was a welcome relief as it slid down his parched throat, a soothing balm against the dryness. There was a slight tang to the water, but it seemed safe enough to drink.

Without further thought, Jack took the backpack off his shoulders and opened it to find the almost empty water bottle within. He uncapped it and took the last mouthful of water it contained and dunked it into the small pool. He filled it to the brim before he leaned against the wall nearby to rest and took more gulps from the bottle, sighing in satisfaction as he did so.

Moments later, an odd tingling sensation began to spread through his body. A slow, simmering nausea gripped his insides, refusing to let go. The cave spun wildly, his vision blurring into streaks of color, and a cold sweat broke out on his skin as the dizziness intensified. He tried to steady himself, but his legs gave way, and he sank to the ground beside the pool.

As he lay there, the cool stone pressing against his cheek, his eyelids grew heavy. Despite his efforts to stay awake, a deep, unnatural drowsiness overcame him. The last thing he saw before slipping into unconsciousness was the gentle ripple of the pool's surface as the trickle of water continued to feed it, travelling in its endless journey over the moss down the cavern walls.

Chapter Twenty-Six
Christina

Christina stumbled through the large cavern, tears streaming down her face, both from the pain of the rocks rubbing against the wounds from her journey through the gap and the loss of Jenny and Adam. Though she didn't know Adam well, she could tell he was a nice guy, and seeing him get torn apart by the person he had fallen for was horrific.

She swung the fading torchlight around her wildly, searching for any sign of where the others had gone, but saw no telltale glow from their flashlights.

Given how little battery remained in her flashlight, she couldn't afford to delay. She needed to keep moving. It was also just a matter of time before that... thing Jenny had become would be after her, too.

Deciding the most logical thing to do was to stick to the walls in hopes of finding a passage, she jogged toward the cave wall just within the distance of her flashlight's beam. Following it, she stumbled over the rocks along the way. Despite trying to avoid them, her reflexes were slow and clumsy, the biting pain of her wounds making her movements awkward and uncoordinated.

The cave wall began to curve in front of her, and then her flashlight fell on a large space darker than the surrounding area. It was a passage; it had to be!

She increased her pace and saw to her relief that her suspicion was correct. There was an opening ahead, and it was large enough for her to enter without any fear of doing further damage by squeezing between its walls.

With a sudden, deafening roar, an explosion of rocks erupted behind her, sending shards of stone flying. She spun around, her eyes wide with fear, just in time to hear the whoosh of enormous wings slicing through the air. The thing must've found some weakness in the wall to burst through so easily like that.

The flapping of wings grew louder and closer until a loud thud announced the creature's landing. It seemed its wings weren't strong enough to bear its weight for long. A heavy thump of footsteps followed soon after, heading in her direction.

The creature was closing in fast, homing in on her torchlight as it let out a terrifying, strained shriek, the sound a cross between Jenny's scream and something primal and animal. Thoughts whirled through Christina's mind as she swung the flashlight around. She could take the passage to her left, but uncertainty gripped her—would it lead to safety or a dead end?

Continuing to scan her immediate surroundings in panic, her light fell upon a huge boulder, partially obscured by shadows. Without a second thought, Christina switched off the flashlight, ran blindly toward it, and darted behind it, pressing her back against its cold, rough surface. She held her breath, her pulse galloping like a runaway horse, as the beast's footsteps grew louder and more menacing.

Approaching the area where she had switched off her flashlight, the creature came to a halt. She could hear its raspy breaths and snuffles as it tried to detect her presence with its sense of smell. She could only hope that the monster's new senses and body were still too new, too uncoordinated to detect things accurately. The sound of shale and small rocks crunching beneath the creature's heavy talons echoed through the cave as it spun, continuing its search. With an angry, screeching sound like nails on a chalkboard, the thing headed towards the passage Christina had seen, its rapid footsteps pounding against the earth before fading into the distance. Christina sighed and allowed herself to suck in some deep breaths in relief.

She now had another decision in front of her. Should she go down the same passage as the creature or look for another one somewhere in this huge cavern? She definitely didn't want to run into that thing, but her flashlight was dying, and she couldn't use her phone as she needed to conserve what little battery it had left in hopes of getting some reception.

She decided to wait and bide her time to see if the monstrosity came back. For all she knew, that passage led to a dead end. She would wait for a while until she was satisfied it wasn't coming back. She switched on the flashlight long enough to find somewhere to sit and settled down to wait, switching it off once more. Her thoughts turned to Jack, Sarah, and Mason, and she prayed that the creature wouldn't find them.

Chapter Twenty-Seven
Mason

Mason opened his eyes groggily and sat up shivering. His clothing was soaked, and the chill of the air had seeped in, making his teeth chatter. His feet were still dangling in the water, but something beyond them caught his eye. He had to blink a couple of times to clear the sleep from his eyes to realize what it was. It was the severed bottom half of Sarah bobbing near the centre of the pool. Bits of dangling intestine, tendons, and torn flesh were hanging loose and disappeared beneath the surface.

Mason felt his gorge rise, and he turned to his side, evacuating the contents of his stomach onto the damp, rugged floor of the cavern. His mind reeled, haunted by Sarah's mangled body and the horrifying creature responsible. Whatever it had been seemed familiar somehow. Then it hit him. It was seemingly impossible, but it had borne a strong resemblance to the mythic lake monster that was rumoured to inhabit the nearby Lake Champlain. If it was that thing, then the pool in the cavern must be connected to the lake somehow. The creature was said to have been around for hundreds of years. He even had a goddamn fluffy toy replica of it. What was it called again... Champ? He made a mental note to throw it out when he got home. Home, a place where Sarah would never be again. Pulling his feet from the water, he hugged his knees to his chest and rocked, overcome by renewed sobs.

A sudden, distant, angry shriek pulled his attention away from his grief, and Mason wiped his eyes as he stared back towards the cavern's mouth. He only just had time to wonder whether it was the same shriek that Jack had been talking about before rhythmic thudding grew audible in the distance. He strained his ears, trying to work out what it was, before he realized how fast it was moving toward him. He shot to his feet, wincing as his muscles, stiff with cold, protested. There was no doubt about it, those were footsteps, but not from any human.

He ran towards the opening in the cave they had first seen on arrival before stopping at its mouth, remembering the flashlight Sarah had abandoned before lust had consumed them. He changed directions, conscious of the growing volume of the footsteps, and sprinted toward the boulder. Skidding to a stop, he scooped up the flashlight before smoothly reversing direction toward the tunnel. It was times like these that he was thankful for his football skills. As he reached the opening, he switched on his flashlight, the weak beam cutting through the darkness ahead. His feet found a steady rhythm as the cold wore off; a rush of blood and the familiar power that had saved his football team countless times surging through his legs.

With ease, Mason navigated the scattered rocks on the cave floor, his movements deliberate, forceful, honed by years of battling through defensive lines. He lost himself to the moment, imagining he was back on the football field, the pounding footsteps behind him like those of an approaching blitz. Every step was controlled, each shift of weight precise, his footwork disciplined as he cut past jagged rock formations like he was forcing open a gap in the defensive line. He adjusted his stance to widen it, keeping his body low, absorbing the uneven terrain and driving forward with sheer determination. Then reality kicked in once more as he reached the exit into a cavern larger than any he had come across before and came to a halt.

Sections of the huge space were illuminated by the similar glow of the moss he had seen in the chamber he had fled from. From what he could make out, this cavern was at least as large as one of the larger football stadiums used by the NFL. The ceiling over him glittered faintly from minerals and hung imposingly high, almost as high as the length of the cavern itself. Portions of it were populated by stalactites, dangling menacingly downward like accusatory fingers pointing towards him.

As he swept the dim beam of his flashlight across the ground, he caught sight of jagged stalagmites jutting up from the floor, their sharp points only just visible in the faint light. They stood like silent sentinels, their rough surfaces glistening with moisture.

Mason took a cautious step forward, the crunch of loose stone underfoot echoing in the cavernous space. Besides his footsteps, the only other sound was the distant drip of water, a reminder of the slow, relentless passage of time that had shaped this subterranean world. He paused, stunned by the surreal beauty of the scene. The sheer scale of the chamber made Mason feel insignificant, like an ant in a giant's world.

The pounding footsteps from behind once again came into earshot. He'd managed to put some space between himself and whatever it was behind, but the pause had given it a chance to regain ground.

"Shit," Mason mumbled, turning his attention to what

lay ahead of him. The flashlight beam flickered, its light dimming further. He gave it a quick shake, and the beam strengthened once more. Not wasting any more time, he set off toward the other side of the cavern. That way lay in darkness, but at least if he went straight, he could roughly tell where he had come from if he needed to return.

Mason jogged through the forest of stalagmites, each step he took deliberate to avoid the smaller jagged formations that jutted up from the ground. His torchlight flickered weakly, casting eerie shadows that danced on the ground. The air grew thicker, carrying with it a pungent, musty odor that made him wrinkle his nose in distaste.

Mason noticed the ground beneath his feet becoming softer and more uneven. He glanced down and realized he was treading on a floor laden with guano, the accumulated droppings of countless bats that had made this cave their home. The realization sent a ripple of unease through him as he recalled what they had done to Christina and Jenny, but he pressed on, conscious of the thing pursuing him.

Suddenly, a rustling erupted from nearby, growing louder and more frantic. Mason's heart raced as he looked up, just in time to see a horde of bats dropping from their roosts on the ceiling above the stalagmites he was jogging through. The air was filled with the sound of flapping wings and high-pitched squeaks, the bats swirling around him in a chaotic frenzy.

Mason ducked and covered his head, trying to shield himself from the onslaught. The cavern, once silent and still, had erupted into a whirlwind of motion and noise. Mason knew he had to find a way out before the bats' protests turned into something more dangerous, especially if these were the same type that had attacked Jenny and Christina.

"Fuck, fuck, fuck!" he yelled in panic, failing to realize

that his cries might agitate the bats further and draw more attention from what was pursuing him.

He cleared the stalagmite-laden area, and an open stretch of cavern floor lay in front of him. The bats continued to swarm above him, dive bombing toward him and screeching angrily. As he concentrated on each step, waving his arms to fend off the bats that swooped down, he noticed the ground was rising. Soon, he was scrambling up an increasingly steep slope, the rough stones digging into his hands and knees. By some miracle, none of the bats had made contact with him yet, but he knew it was only a matter of time. Before he knew it, he had reached the top, but his momentum was too great to stop, and he found himself spilling back down the other side. His muscles screamed in agony with each tumble over the unforgiving stony terrain. Loose rocks and pebbles cascaded down along with him, creating a mini avalanche that carried him downward until he tumbled to a stop, his body a patchwork of cuts and bruises. Panting, he lay there stunned, staring upward at the never-ending darkness above him. He was afraid to move, fearing that something might have broken in the fall, but there was no choice. He could hear the angry shrieks of the bats nearby. If they found him again, he was in no shape to defend himself. He needed time to assess his injuries and plan his next steps.

Raising his head off the ground gingerly, he examined himself, half expecting to see one of his limbs bent the wrong way. He was relieved to find everything seemed to be in the right place. As a bonus, he still had the flashlight gripped in his right hand, and it was still operational, though it was dimmer than before. He wiggled his toes and fingers. Those were fine too. He sat up cautiously, trying to remain silent. He felt the loose rocks and pebbles shift beneath his feet, each tiny movement a potential giveaway to his whereabouts. The urgency of the situation pressed down on him, but he moved slowly, wincing and gritting his teeth against the sharp pains that shot through him as he stood.

"Shit," he whispered to himself. If he was bleeding, and he was sure he was, then it didn't matter how quiet he moved, the bats would detect the scent. Or would they? He hesitated, questioning whether they would or not, but he had no way of knowing what type of bats these were. He needed to find shelter and find it now.

Turning his back on the slope of rocks he had tumbled down, he scanned the area ahead with the flashlight, cursing to himself when he saw how weak the glow was. To his relief, he could see what looked like a depression within the cave wall ahead. He had to hope it would be enough cover for him to plan out his next move in peace.

He staggered in that direction, feeling his muscles cry out in protest. A palpable tension hung in the air with every movement; the silence was broken only by the frantic beating of his own heart, each pulse a countdown to the expected whoosh of diving bats. He breathed a little easier when he arrived and nestled into the darkest corner of the depression to make himself the smallest possible target and immediately switched off the flashlight to preserve what little battery remained.

Chapter Twenty-Eight
Christina

Christina groaned as she slowly rose to her feet. A sharp pain, like a burning brand, ripped through her back; ignoring it, she gritted her teeth, straightened, and flicked on her flashlight.

As dim as the beam was, it still took her a few moments to blink away the sudden rush of light after being entrenched in darkness for so long. An hour had passed since the creature had disappeared into the passage, and there had been no sign of it since. The time constraint to find an escape was lifted, at least as far as Jenny's health was concerned, but now they had to contend with whatever the fuck she had turned into.

"Out of the frying pan and into the fire," Christina muttered to herself, shaking her head.

She began to walk toward the passage, staring at the dim glow of her flashlight before her, when a thought struck, and she stopped in her tracks. If she went into the passage, she had no way of knowing where it would lead and how long it would take to find an exit, if there even was one. Or the others, for that matter. Her flashlight, as weak as the glow indicated, was unlikely to last long. Now that the creature had gone and had, in theory, smashed a hole through the cave where they had come in from, maybe she could find another flashlight in one of the backpacks Adam had discarded. A shiver, cold and sharp, passed through her at the thought of seeing Adam, or what might remain of him, and her stomach twisted with dread. Even so, she was in no condition to be careless; the weak beam of her flashlight was all that stood between her and utter darkness, and the battery was almost dead.

With the decision made, she turned and headed back toward the area where the creature had come from. A few minutes later, she came across the piles of scattered rocks that had been blasted out from the creature's emergence. She turned toward the wall and studied the hole before her.

It was wide and uneven and looked like it could collapse at any second. Chunks of rock were scattered around like the remnants of a shattered fortress, but she decided it was worth the risk. If she took her time and didn't brush against any of the rocks on either side of the hole as she passed through, it should be safe enough. Or at least she hoped so.

She approached the entrance, trying to be as light on her feet as she could. Her limbs felt leaden and unresponsive, each movement clumsy and awkward. Usually nimble and agile, she wasn't used to the heavy feeling her body had taken on since her back injury. Still, despite a few close calls when she became unbalanced after avoiding the chunks of rock on the ground, she made it through to the other side without incident.

With a soft sigh of relief, she paused to take her bearings, moving the flashlight around her slowly. She had entered a few feet away from the gap she had squeezed through that had wrought havoc on her back. The wall the creature had made a hole through was significantly thinner than the wall where the gap was. Somehow, the monstrosity formerly known as Jenny must've been able to detect that it was the easiest place to break through.

Chills snaked down her spine. The knowledge that the creature wasn't just a mindless beast, but was capable of rational thought and decision making, terrified her. It made the surviving group's situation exponentially more dangerous.

Taking a deep breath, steeling herself against the grim sight she knew awaited, she swung the torchlight toward the backpacks, catching a glimpse of Adam's remains despite her best efforts to avoid them. The ground was awash with chunks of his bloody flesh, surrounded by pools of dark, thick blood. Her arm, holding the flashlight, trembled violently, casting dancing, grotesque shadows on the cave walls as a wave of nausea threatened to overcome her. With great difficulty, the weak glow of the jittery torchlight finally settled on the familiar lumps of the backpacks. The stench of blood was overwhelming as she picked her way toward them, carefully avoiding the scattered, bloody clumps of what was once Adam.

Swallowing hard, she fought back the nausea as the coppery tang of blood filled her nostrils. Pinching her nose shut, she looked at Jenny's backpack, deciding it was her best bet for a spare flashlight. Grabbing it, she rifled through its contents and found one. With a flick of the switch, the bright beam of the flashlight sprang to life. She felt an intense relief; the strong glow was a welcome sight and an indication that its battery was almost full. Trembling, she grabbed her backpack, a frown creasing her face at its surprising lightness. She opened it and found only a few bags of crisps; no sign of the water bottle she had packed. Frantically, she searched through the other backpacks, locating the water bottles in Adam's pack; she snatched a few, tossing them and her almost depleted, switched-off flashlight into her own bag. She left the other backpacks on the ground as she turned around, desperate to flee the horrific scene.

With a backpack in one hand and a flashlight in the other, she made her way through the mess on wobbly legs. Laser-focused on the exit, her foot landed on something squishy with a sickening squelch. A strangled gulp fell unbidden from her mouth as she glanced down to see Adam's arm, partially severed, mangled, and lying beneath her foot, the raw flesh exposed and pulpy. She raised her leg, but his flesh, still clinging, swung back and forth like a grotesque pendulum performing a macabre dance in the air.

Gagging, she set her foot down, this time unable to hold back the flood of vomit as it erupted from her mouth and splashed onto the floor, adding to the already over-whelming coppery stench of blood in the small, confined space.

She shivered, her body weak from the trauma it had gone through during the events of the night, and continued toward the exit. Adam's flesh stubbornly clung to her foot, creating a sickening, wet splat sound with every spongy step. Christina struggled to contain her heaving insides. Just before she reached the unstable-looking exit, she gingerly raised her foot and scraped off Adam's flesh on a chunk of rock on the ground. She winced as it came loose and fell to the floor with a soft slap. The nausea returned with a vengeance, and she dry heaved, her stomach already empty from the previous bout of vomiting.

"Fuck this place," she whispered and made her way as quickly as she could through the exit and back out into the comparatively fresher air of the cavern beyond. Swinging left, she walked a few meters along the wall, stopping to breathe in the earthy, mineral-rich scent—a welcome change from the stench of blood and death lingering in the cavern she'd just escaped from.

A few moments and cleansing sips of water later, she set off towards the passage. Flashes of the horrible scene she had just left plagued her mind, but she forced them away. If she was lucky enough to sleep again, they could haunt her nightmares later.

She entered the passage and followed it. Before long, she could feel a slight breeze swirling toward her, and she took the opportunity to breathe it in, feeling the tension in her stomach ease with each breath she took.

Her progress was slower than she liked; each step sent a fresh wave of pain jolting down her spine, but she was getting used to it. Soon, the passage began to slope gently upward; a stronger breeze cooled her face as a faint glow appeared ahead. She emerged into a large cavern and paused to take it all in. Moss, glowing a soft green color, was the source of the light in the cavern, which was strong enough that Christina didn't need the flashlight. She switched it off and briefly surveyed the scene ahead of her. A large, serene body of water was in the centre of the cavern; before it lay a few large boulders blocking much of the view. If she had time, she would have allowed herself to be wowed by what she was seeing, but time was something she did not have. She needed to find the others. She scanned the walls searching for an exit and found one in the cave wall, left of the pool of water.

Anxious to move on, she walked toward the new passage, giving passing glances toward the water and the boulders in front, and there her gaze fell upon something that made her blood run cold. Articles of Sarah's clothing were strewn around the area immediately in front of the boulder.

"Oh, fuck fuck fuck, no," Christina murmured, her chest pounding as she walked as fast as her ruined back would allow toward the discarded clothing. Approaching it, she frowned, puzzled. To her relief, there were no signs of blood, and nothing was torn; it was just dirty as one would expect after navigating through the cave system. But still, what was it doing here? Where was Sarah? Every article of clothing she had been wearing was here, including her undergarments. Could she and Mason have stopped here to go skinny dipping? If so, why were Sarah's clothes still here?

She swivelled around slowly, careful not to jolt her back as she scanned all corners of the cavern. There were no signs of either Sarah or Mason. Confused, she walked around the boulders, looking at the entirety of the lake. Her eyes widened in horror when she saw it—lying in the water was a grotesque, twisted string of entrails that had spilled out of the floating mass of flesh beside it. It was a woman's naked bottom half, severed just below the waist. The ragged flesh, swollen and discolored from the water, revealed dull reddish meat and organs, the blood that was once contained within now spread throughout the water it lay in. She knew just by the legs alone that it belonged to Sarah. They dangled in the water, untouched, still as perfect as they had always been, once the admiration of many, now destined to rot in a cavern and never be seen by human eyes again.

"Oh god, Sarah, no!" she said, and turned away, clutching her stomach. She fought the urge to retch but ultimately failed, expelling the watery mixture she had left in her stomach onto the ground.

She stumbled back, her head reeling, her mind filled with the vision of the macabre sight. Though it wasn't as gruesome as the scene of Adam's demise, this felt worse. This was Sarah, her best friend. The one she woke up to a message from every day. The one who always had her back.

The one she had essentially grown into an adult with since freshman year, now gone forever.

Tears streamed down her face as she leant back on the boulder behind her, her body trembling once more, this time with grief. The pain of loss kicked in, and it was overwhelming, a raw, aching void that threatened to consume her. Thoughts of their shared past filled her head. The pair of them laughing together, bright and joyful, the weight of secrets they'd held close, and the sweet hope of dreams they'd held dear. Their adventures together, from dazzling nights out to cozy girls' nights in, and the electrifying performances they created in cheerleading, now relegated to nothing more than thought and recollection.

The weight of her sadness pressed down on her, stealing away her awareness of time. A faint shout, echoing from the passage, pierced her misery, pulling her back to reality. It sounded like Mason. She straightened up and wiped her eyes with a shaky hand, leaving a muddy trail across her tear-streaked face. Standing still for a few minutes, she strained her ears, listening for another cry, but all she heard was the drumming of her own heart.

She sniffled and tried to compose herself. Sarah might be gone, but it sounded like Mason was still alive, and if that shout was any indication, he needed help. She walked toward the passage on shaky legs. If that Jenny creature thing had done this, Christina wasn't sure what she could do, even if she wasn't as injured as she was, but she wasn't going to stand by while she lost another of her dwindling number of friends.

Chapter Twenty-Nine
Jack

Jack woke with a gasp, immediately feeling sharp pangs shooting through his stomach. It felt like he was being stabbed repeatedly by invisible knives, and he could do nothing to stop it. He doubled over with a strangled moan as he clawed at his stomach, his body wracked with a pain so intense it stole his breath. With desperation fuelling his actions, he thrust his fingers down his throat until the violent spasm of his gag reflex finally released the pressure. An eruption of watery, foul-smelling liquid burst from his mouth onto the ground, and almost immediately, his pain eased from unbearable to tolerable. He leaned back, breathing slowly and cautiously. His stomach felt raw and ravaged, a dull ache replacing the razor-sharp pain that had plagued it.

He glanced down at his watch and was surprised to see barely an hour had passed, the green glow of his watch face ticking just over the 3:00 am mark. Still, it was time he couldn't afford to waste when the others were counting on him. Staring at the discarded water bottle next to him in disgust, he uncapped it and poured its remaining contents onto the ground before screwing the cap back on and placing it in his backpack. Hopefully, he could make do without water until he found a way out. He didn't think he could trust another water source, even if he found one after this experience.

With an agonized groan, he heaved himself to his feet, his hand gripping the lip of the tainted water pool as his other hand clung to his backpack. The air was thick with the smell of his vomit and the polluted water he'd spewed on the ground. Wincing in discomfort, he slung the backpack over his shoulder and reached down to pick up the flashlight.

With the uncharted passage as his target, he entered, switched on his flashlight, and paused to survey what was ahead of him. This tunnel, at least, was wider than the ones he had come through so far. He began to walk down it, albeit slower than he would have liked. His stomach still throbbed with a dull ache, punctuated by sharp, sudden pains serving as harsh reminders of his foolishness. He could only hope that he didn't have to do any running or strenuous activity until it calmed down.

A few minutes later, he emerged onto a platform overlooking a gigantic cavern, and his heart sank even as his eyes widened with wonder. Immediately before him was the remains of a man-made rope bridge. Several massive, rotting wooden posts, their wood crumbling and stained with age, were driven into the earth on either side of the gaping chasm before him. On the post nearest the edge, the remnants of a thick rope, frayed and worn, hung precariously; its ends vanishing into the shadowy abyss below. The opposite post showed only a faded, weathered mark where the rope had once been. He shined the flashlight on the chasm's far side, where a few decaying, moss-covered boards lay scattered. It was out of his reach, the gap too large to leap across.

"Goddamn it," he yelled, his frustration almost palpable. Now what the fuck was he supposed to do? He had come all this way for nothing—wasting his time, and worse, the time of those counting on him. He felt like such a failure, and it was a feeling he wasn't used to. He was supposed to be the dependable one, always there to make the crucial play on the football field or lend a hand when physical strength was needed. Ok, sure, he'd needed to rely on Christina and Adam academically, but that was the exception. And here? Here, he should have been in his element. He was Jack, no physical obstacle was too great to overcome. Except he'd met his match. Right here and now, when he was needed most.

"Fuck, fuck, fuuuuuuck!" he screamed, cupping his hands around his mouth to amplify his voice, letting the world know he was pissed off. A distant, angry-sounding crack of rocks sent him stumbling backward in panic. Then came a massive snap, and the air filled with the echoing thunder of a rockslide.

He slumped against the wall beside the cavern's dark mouth, the rough texture scratching his back as he slid to the ground. Pulling his knees to his chest, he surrendered to his self-pity. Sobs wracked his already pained stomach, and suddenly he began to feel each and every bruise, scratch, and tear on his skin.

Weariness filled him, a deep sense of hopelessness pervading through his very being. Then came the shame and self-loathing, things that only he knew bore for himself, although Christina had seen glimpses at times in the aftermath of his team's worst losses. The things he feared most —his vulnerability, his inner turmoil—were weaknesses he couldn't conquer. He had worked hard to build a strong, confident, and even arrogant exterior so he could fit in. So he could be seen as unstoppable and reliable. Inside though. Inside was a different matter. He was terrified. Terrified of letting people down. That he wasn't good enough. That his next play or move would end in failure. Worst of all, terrified that he would hurt or fail Christina. And that was exactly what he had done.

Tears flowed freely from his eyes. The emotions felt endless, a dam of pent-up feelings finally breaking, overwhelming and unstoppable. Then he heard it. An indistinct, high-pitched, desperate yell, thin and reedy with panic.

"Mason?" Jack murmured, questioning the reality of what he was hearing.

He scrambled to his feet, wiping his blurred eyes free of tears, and directed his flashlight down over the edge of the platform. To his surprise, he could see a dim glow in the distance and a figure jumping up and down, waving its hands at him and pointing at something above.

"...ck... un..."

"What the fuck are you saying?" he yelled back before he stopped, puzzled by the sudden whooshing sound he heard from above.

"Jack, run!" Mason's words suddenly became clearer as Jack shone his flashlight upwards, its beam landing on something from his worst nightmares. At first glance, it looked like a gigantic bat. The glare from his torch revealed a strange glow as it fell on its body, which he realized was the light shining through its translucent, almost ethereal skin. It was headed right towards him. All pretence of stealth gone, the creature shrieked, its high-pitched wail piercing the air, and for a moment, Jack could have sworn it sounded like a woman's scream.

"What the fuck is that?" Jack said, stumbling back

towards the passage, before he turned and started running down it. A few short steps later, he stopped and froze in fear. The sound of huge, familiar footfalls, those which he had heard on the other side of the dead end, were pounding toward him. An answering shriek, much more animalistic and deep, reverberated from the passage in front of him. Jack's heart stopped, panic, terror, and indecision filling him. The crushing weight of his predicament bore down on him. *This is it, I'm going to die*, he thought, the words echoing in his mind before the sting of his own slap jolted him back to reality. He couldn't give up this easily. He turned around and bolted back the way he came, skidding to a halt at the small platform, directing his flashlight downward, hoping that by some miracle, a way out would present itself to him. To his relief, he found the leftmost corner of the platform dropped down onto a ledge overlooking a sloping hill that led, he presumed, to the cave floor. His flashlight was not able to reach it from his position to verify.

He gritted his teeth, preparing for the inevitable sound of the huge bat-like creature swooping toward him as he rushed toward the ledge. Upon reaching it, he frowned in confusion. The sound was growing fainter, not louder. He chanced a brief swing of his flashlight beam toward the direction of the fading whooshes of its large wings. The beast was heading toward Mason, who was now out in the open, screaming, whooping, and jumping, trying to attract its attention.

"Thank you, bro," Jack breathed, swinging his legs over the lip of the platform, aligning himself with the ledge below before dropping down. Above him, the heavy footfalls were getting closer.

"Shit, shit, shit" he muttered, swinging the flashlight

wildly beneath him to search for the safest place to drop down to next.

Below, on the ground, Mason began to run awkwardly towards the furthest side of the cavern, a limp apparent in his movements, before disappearing into another passage. The creature in pursuit dropped down to the floor and ran in after him.

Spotting an area that looked easier to navigate than the rest, he swung himself over the ledge onto the tall mound of rocks and began to make his way down it hurriedly. The footfalls stopped above, followed by an inhuman screech of anger. He increased his speed, adding a touch more risk to his journey downwards, but made it to the bottom just as the whoosh of wings sounded from above, signifying the creature's pursuit. Not pausing to stop, Jack ran on, putting his speed and stamina from his days on the field to good use, towards the opposite end of the cavern where Mason had disappeared. He might be crazy to run after one of the fucking things while another one was hot on his heels —but there was no way he'd let Mason down; he'd failed everyone already tonight and wasn't about to do it again.

Chapter Thirty

Mason

Mason knew as soon as he saw that thing and Jack appear almost simultaneously that he had to do something. The creature, a huge, ugly bat-like monstrosity that looked like a gigantic version of those creepy fucking bats that had kept him company, was obviously the thing that had been chasing him. If there was any doubt, it was swept away by its shriek, identical to the one he'd heard in the cavern with the lake. It had been the first to spot Jack, its senses more attuned to the cave than Mason was. Mason had followed the direction of its gaze to find the figure of Jack, illuminated by his flashlight high above him in the distance, in an area where Mason's dying flashlight could never have reached.

Attracted by his distant screams, the creature had unfurled its giant fleshy wings and flapped them furiously. It had at first struggled to get off the ground but eventually succeeded and flew toward Jack.

That was when Mason had stood up, switched on his almost dead flashlight, and dared to stand out in the open, daunting darkness of the cavern.

Now, as he screamed, waved, and jumped up and down, his stiff legs protesting with each jarring launch, he began to question his decision. He had no plan beyond just trying to get the fucking thing away from Jack. Luckily for him, the bats that had been circling above the depression he had hidden in were nowhere to be seen, so at least that danger was gone. Maybe they'd been scared off by big momma—or was it big papa? Hard to say. How do you even tell the gender of these things, anyway? It's not like they came with a label.

Finally, his antics caught the creature's attention. The beast paused its advance toward Jack and turned around clumsily mid-air to face him.

"That's right, you fuckin' overgrown furry potato with wings, come get me. I've seen better flying skills from a paper bag," he yelled out, keeping an eye on Jack's flashlight glow from up above as it began to disappear back the way it came. "Come on, you giant flying prune, what are you—"

The creature let out a shriek that drowned out his sentence and began to descend toward him. Mason's stomach plunged as he turned around in the opposite direction and began to run.

"Oh fuck, I've done it now. Probably should have found a way out first before I pissed it off," he muttered, wincing with each step he took. The fall must've tweaked something aside from just giving him the initial bruises and cuts he thought he had.

"Well shit, that's not going to help with Sunday's game now is it? Or is it tomorrow? Fuck knows what time it is now," he murmured, glancing behind him to see nothing but darkness. Of course, he couldn't see anything; what little torchlight he had was trained on the ground in front of him. In the direction he should be focusing on.

His flashlight flickered weakly, and he bashed it with his

hands, willing it to stay on. The hit seemed to brighten the light somewhat, but who knew how long it would last. Behind him, the flapping of large, leathery wings grew closer. A heavy whooshing, like the rush of wind, filled the air, followed by a resounding thud as the creature landed.

He had almost reached the cave wall in front of him now, and his eyes widened in welcome relief when he saw the telltale patch of darkness that indicated another passage. For all he knew, it could lead to a dead end, but he had no choice. The sound of heavy footfalls urged him onwards, and he ran into the opening without hesitation, keeping his eyes focused on the small patch of light provided by the flashlight ahead of him.

Following the tunnel's twists and turns, his fear began to mount as his adrenaline wore off. The creature was matching his pace, and he wasn't losing it as he had hoped. His speed was severely hampered by the injury he'd sustained, which he was beginning to think was something to do with his hamstring. Not only that, but it felt like it was getting worse.

Ahead of him, the tunnel branched into two passages. Mason skidded to a halt, his eyes darting between the two options. The left passage was narrow and twisted, disappearing into the shadows. The right passage was wider but sloped steeply downward, the ground uneven and treacherous.

He hesitated, torn between the choices. The pounding footsteps of the creature reminded him that he couldn't afford to waste any more time. His mind raced, weighing the risks. The narrow passage might slow the monster down, but it could also trap him if it was a dead end. The wider passage offered more space to manoeuvre, but it sloped downward away from the surface, the opposite direction he needed to go.

Fear clawed at his mind, threatening to overwhelm him. He glanced down at his flashlight, the light growing weaker with each passing second. The battery was almost dead, and soon he would be plunged into complete darkness. Panic surged through him, but he forced himself to stay focused.

He chose the left passage and entered its labyrinthine depths. Though it was narrow, it was just wide enough for him to move in without scraping against the rocks. He was moving significantly slower, but he hoped the small passage would do the same to his pursuer, maybe even bring it to a halt.

Behind him, he heard the heavy footfalls come to a stop, followed by a piercing screech that sounded curiously human-like near its end. It was a shriek filled with a horrifying blend of agony and predatory hunger.

Mason kept moving; the creature might not be able to squeeze through the passage after him, but it might know where it ended and meet him there. He needed to get as far away from that thing as he could.

He emerged into another branching passageway; this time, both directions looked similar, but one sloped upward slightly. He chose the one that he hoped more likely led toward the surface and continued on. It wasn't long before the passages began to branch with increasing regularity, and each time, he chose the one that either had fresher air, a slight breeze, or an upward slant. He had no time to study his options further; the light on his flashlight was almost down to nothing. It was just after making one of these choices, and he'd begun his trek into the chosen passage, when the flashlight died completely. There was no amount of shaking, banging, or pleading that made it turn on again. It was dead. As dead as his chances had now become. He felt the heavy weight of despair wash over him as the slight sliver of hope he had left disappeared into the darkness he was now lost in.

"Fuck it," he murmured. "If I'm going to die, at least I died saving Jack. At least I think I did. You better be alive, Jack, you big bastard."

Alone and in utter darkness, he found himself sinking further into his despondency. Thoughts of his parents filled his mind. Would they even notice he was gone? Probably not for a while. Days could pass, maybe more, before anyone questioned his absence, unless one of the others made it out, and told them. And his brother? If anything, his brother might be relieved. One less argument. One less reminder of everything they never saw eye to eye on. That kind of silence had already stretched between them for months. Maybe now, it would stretch forever.

He exhaled, slow and quiet. Even time felt distant down here. What time was it, anyway? He instinctively raised his wrist towards his eye, and a slight glow materialized as his smartwatch activated. It was 4:34 am. Wait a minute... He still had his watch!

"You're a fucking idiot," he said to himself, feeling a sudden surge of relief. How the hell had he not realized it was there before? Probably because he'd been so used to wearing it that he no longer spared it a thought. He checked the battery. It was on 14%. Better than nothing. He accessed the watch's menu and activated its flashlight function.

"Back in business, for now at least," he said.

Thankful for the temporary reprieve, he ventured onward, the sound of his echoing footsteps his only companion. This particular tunnel seemed to stretch on forever. His injured leg, at least, certainly made it feel that way. In reality, only ten minutes had passed. A few more moments later, all thoughts of time and the pain from his leg were forgotten as he entered into a small cavern that took his breath away. His eyes widened in wonder as he took in the otherworldly soft, blue-green light that bathed the cavern in a celestial luminescence. The light came from glowworms; their tiny forms lit up as if they were miniature stars that had decided to settle in this hidden underground world.

"Oh, Sarah, if only you were here to see this," he said, feeling tears well at the corners of his eyes.

It took him a moment to notice there was a large rock formation to his right at the end of the cavern. Its shape resembled that of a natural altar of sorts, but his gaze was drawn to something beside it. Something that didn't belong, with a metallic glint. His tears came to a halt when he realized it was an old, rusted mining sign embedded above a small passage at the other end of the cavern. He staggered towards it, feeling hope rise once more.

There was writing on the sign, but it wasn't legible, its letters worn and corroded by time and the damp air that pervaded the cavern, but it didn't matter. It represented freedom, bringing with it the promise of fresh air, sunlight, and... a shower... he thought to himself as he caught wind of the unmistakable stench of his unwashed body.

As he neared the middle of the cavern, he felt his hairs raise at the back of his neck. There was something strange about that rock formation; it felt... wrong somehow. The glowworms illuminated the cave, but this area was an exception; an unnatural absence of light created a dark void. It was as if there was some sort of invisible wall there, steering the glowworms away from the area. Behind the rock formation itself was darkness and a slight waft of warmth and decay, a stark contrast from the earthy smell that the rest of the cavern contained. Despite his unease, it was right beside the passage with the sign above it, and he needed to get past it.

He focused on the passage ahead, but his eyes were drawn to the rock formation that looked increasingly like an altar, until he stopped a few feet away, his mouth open in shock. Now that he was closer to it, he could see it was composed of smooth, layered stone. Its surface, slick with moisture, shimmered faintly with a dull, wet sheen, from what little ambient light managed to reach it. The base of the formation was broad and solid, tapering upwards to a flat, wide top that resembled a ceremonial table.

On that table was the unmistakable discoloration of dried blood, caked in layers that spoke of countless contributions. It looked to him like it was some sort of sacrificial altar. A waft of fresh air from above blew away the scent of decay and drew his attention. There was a hole in the ceiling which appeared to open out to the surface. He could see the indistinct shapes of roots along the edges and the dim twinkling of stars, almost lost in the brighter glow of the cave's glowworms.

Could it be someone was providing sacrifices to this thing that had been chasing him? For what purpose?

A sudden, wet snuffling pierced his thoughts, followed by an ear-splitting shriek that sent a jolt of icy terror through him, stopping his heart in his chest. The creature stepped out of the shadows behind the altar. Its eyes glowed with eerie bioluminescence, casting a faint, ghostly shimmer in the darkness.

"Oh fuck no," Mason whispered, his eyes wide with horror, as he stumbled backward, his breath catching in his throat. He briefly thought of making a run for the passage next to the altar, but discarded that course almost immediately. The creature would easily intercept him, especially in his current state. The only option left was the way he'd come in. If he made it, hopefully, he could lose it in the maze of passages. A louder, more primal screech from behind him put paid to that idea, too.

"There's two of you giant flying rats? Well, come on then, if you want your snacky snack, I ain't gonna make it easy for you."

Both creatures shrieked in response. Mason redirected himself and backed away towards the wall behind him. He spotted the second creature at the entrance to the passage he had emerged from, and he continued stepping backwards, trying to keep both in view. Despite the bravado in his words, his heart was palpitating wildly. Sweat ran in rivulets down his back, and his skin had turned a pallid grey. With every step he took backwards, the two creatures took one forward, their otherworldly yellow eyes filled with curiosity as they watched him.

He knew that this was most likely his end. He could only stall for time, give the others a chance to escape, and hope his death wouldn't be meaningless—that it would count for something.

Taking another step backward, he felt his foot knock against something solid that spun away from the impact. He froze, and the two creatures stiffened. Their long leathery ears twitched as their snub noses sniffed at the air with wet snuffles. Keeping an eye on the two beasts, he knelt with slow, careful movements until he was within reach of whatever it was next to his foot. Daring a quick glance down, he saw it was a bone roughly the size of his forearm. Without thinking, he scooped it up and stood up slowly. The two creatures looked between him and the bone and began to snarl softly. The larger brute that had emerged from the same tunnel as him exposed its teeth in a show of aggression.

His skin crawled with disgust, knowing that the bone he had in his hand was from no animal; it looked human.

The fleeting thought that he'd actually learned something in anatomy inexplicably filled him with a strange sense of accomplishment before the reality of the situation drew his focus back to the creatures before him.

He kept backing up until the rough cave wall dug into his spine. The monsters stood huffing, their bodies tensed as saliva dripped from the corners of their lips to the ground. With a territorial shriek and a snap of its jaws at the other creature, the larger one charged forward, leaping at Mason in a whirlwind of leathery skin and talons.

Swinging the bone with all his might, Mason managed to make contact with the side of the creature's head with a crack, sending it staggering sideways into the cave wall beside him. The bone snapped in two and fell to the ground in pieces, but it had done its job. The thing's head collided with the wall with a dull thud, and it fell to the ground unmoving. It was either stunned or dead, and Mason didn't wait to find out. He staggered forward, giving the fallen creature a wide berth, only to come face-to-face with the other one. It stood tall before him in the middle of the cavern, waiting for him to either try to get around it or retreat. It was in a prime position to capitalize on both options. Whatever these beasts may be, they certainly weren't dumb.

"Fuck you, whatever you are," he said defiantly before his eyes fell on a scrap of clothing, a piece of black woollen jumper clinging to the creature's shoulder. Mason narrowed his eyes and saw more pieces of it hanging from its torso. In his haste to get away from the thing, he hadn't noticed it before. Then he saw the tattered scraps of denim clinging to the creature's bony inner thigh.

"What the hell?" he whispered, his eyes widening in recognition. "Jenny... that's what Jenny was wearing. But it can't be. You can't be Jenny, there's no way."

The way the creature reacted to hearing Jenny's name made his heart sink and his terror rise simultaneously. In a show of recognition, it cocked its head sideways, its ears twitching, and closed its mouth for a moment; a flash of something—confusion?—came over its eyes before it was replaced by a shriek of pure, unadulterated anger. A faint trace of Jenny's voice in the shriek made Mason recoil in horror.

"Holy shit, Jenny. It's you, isn't it?"

The monster stepped forward and bared its sharp teeth, unfurling its wings in a show of aggression. Mason instantly knew it was going to attack, but that knowledge only served to heighten his fear. He turned toward the passage he entered from and began to run. He had only made it a few steps before a sharp stabbing pain from his shoulder carving its way down to his lower back sent him stumbling and crashing heavily to the floor. His screams of agony rang through the cavern as his body spasmed, trying to come to terms with the trauma of the wound he had suffered.

He could feel blood pouring from the gash on his back and gingerly reached behind him with a shaky hand, feeling the ragged and torn flesh of his shoulder blade, tracing it downwards. He knew instinctively that this was it. With just one swipe, the thing that was Jenny had ended him. A scalding pain, like white hot fire, emanated from his shoulder and upper back, but below it, he strangely couldn't feel anything. It was like the pain ended at his lower back. He tried to wiggle his toes and move his legs, but they remained still, offering no response.

He struggled to draw breaths through the pain and swivelled his head to the side, facing the direction of the creature he had managed to stun or kill, but it was no longer lying there. It was back on its feet and on its way toward him. He had only stunned it then.

As he watched the beasts approach each other, hissing and snarling, he urged himself to make one last effort. He extended his arms, ignoring the agony of his wounds as he dug his fingers into the rough ground ahead of him, pulling himself forward inch by inch.

His breath came in ragged gasps between moans of pain as his body began to weaken. Who knew what damage had been done in that one swipe, but it seemed clear it was destined to lead to his agonizing death. His vision blurred, and only then did he notice the spreading pool of blood around him. Dark spots flickered in his vision, blending with the bioluminescent glow of the cavern's worms. He heaved, muscles straining, but this time he couldn't pull himself forward even an inch. Something was preventing his progress. That something became clear the moment a creature's talons ripped through his throat, its grip like a vise as it hoisted him upward, blood gushing. He hung limply, choking for air, feeling the skin of his pierced neck strain to hold his full body weight as the brute swung him around to face the other, the one that was Jenny, in what seemed to be an offering.

He closed his eyes and pictured Sarah. *I'm coming for you, babe,* he thought as the creature Jenny had become sank its teeth deep into his neck, but Mason was mercifully spared any pain. He was already headed towards the waiting arms of Sarah within the recesses of his fading mind, leaving the monsters to feast on the body he no longer needed.

CHAPTER THIRTY-ONE

The creature revelled in its feast, even as it eyed the other being curiously. This creature felt alien to it, but also familiar. For that matter, so did the delicious thing it was eating, just as the one before it had. The one it had consumed upon becoming what it now was. There was a curious feeling of... what... it couldn't tell, but it felt discomforting. Like its mind was not content with what it was doing, but its body was. Strange images swept through its mind. Images of this thing it was consuming, talking to it, and it, or what it formerly had been, responding in some language it didn't recognize. Confusion plagued its mind like a fog, but it knew it needed sustenance. It knew that the plasma and flesh before it was the nourishment it hungered for.

That other being, the one before it that was staring at it with gleaming, knowing eyes... It was like there was a connection, an unspoken understanding there, and it knew that its path forward belonged with its kind, with the being that stood before it. The being held its gaze as it continued to feast, a hunger of a different kind becoming evident in its eyes as it watched. Another need crept through its mind in response, an urge to ensure the survival of its species, the urge to procreate. It began to understand. It was a female, and the other was a male. The other being's presence was no longer just a source of curiosity; it was a potential mate, a partner in this strange new existence.

The male stood tall, drawing himself up, and something began to drift on the air to her, his scent filling her nostrils and instantly triggering a response. She shifted slightly, her body language indicating her receptiveness. The male, sensing her acceptance, moved closer, his wings enveloping her in a protective embrace. He opened his mouth and gently gripped her neck. Their bond established, the pair prepared to mate, sharing a blend of instinct and mutual understanding. The male mounted her, and the cavern echoed with the sounds of their unnatural courtship.

Once done, they separated, and she immediately felt the urgent need to find a safe place. There was an innate sense that swept over her, that she would bear children, and the future of their race was now dependent on her. Not sparing the male another glance, she took off through the winding passages. She followed her instincts, searching for a place that offered the best chance for a safe birthing ground.

CHAPTER THIRTY-TWO
JACK

Jack sprinted into the passage, switching on his flashlight to illuminate the darkness. The time it took to get there was longer than expected; the distance looked far shorter from where he was originally on the platform. Behind him, he could hear no further signs of pursuit, but he needed to keep his ears open just in case. It was more than likely that the creature following him had been the culprit who had messed with him back in the tunnels earlier and knew where each one would lead. For all he knew, he and Mason could be walking into a trap, but it wasn't like there was any choice.

He wanted to shout out for Mason, but with that thing in here somewhere, he knew he couldn't risk it. Ahead, the passage branched into two, and he skidded to a halt, sweeping his flashlight between the options.

"Fuck!" he said in frustration. Though there were enough rocks to create arrows, he didn't have the time to spare to make one. Mason needed his help and needed it now!

A rapid heartbeat accompanied his struggle to still his

frantic mental whirlwind and think clearly. One passage was a tighter squeeze than the other, which angled downwards. The narrow one would have afforded Mason the better option if he were trying to escape that creature. Given its width, he doubted it would have been able to fit. He headed that way and squeezed in, reminded instantly of the first gap he had gone through. This one at least afforded a little more space, but he still found himself making contact with the walls, his shirt and pants getting caught and tearing in a few places.

Finally, he exited and followed the passage only to find another branching pathway just a short distance in. This time, one curved upward slightly more than the other. He studied the ground, hoping to find some sign that would indicate which way Mason went, but the stony terrain yielded no clues. Tracing footsteps would not work in here.

"If I were Mason, which passage would I take?" he murmured to himself as he glanced between the paths, trying to put himself in Mason's shoes. "Pretty sure you'd take the ones most likely to take you towards the exit. That's what I'd do at least. Please tell me you did, otherwise, we're both fucked," he whispered.

Working off that theory, he opted for the upward sloping path. He sped through the passage, only to find himself facing yet another branch.

"Oh goddamn it," he shouted, the words tumbling out in a torrent of frustration before he clapped a hand over his mouth. If there was any chance the creature didn't know he was following it, then it did now, especially if its hearing was anything like the bats that the thing resembled.

He identified the path he thought Mason would take based on his theory and quickly took it. Each time he encountered a branching passage, his worry increased. The place was like a maze. If Mason was panicked or felt the creature's presence closing in, he could have just as easily chosen a less obvious passage. Jack's confidence eroded with each step, leaving him sure he was lost and had made a wrong choice of direction.

At one point during his journey, he thought he heard the familiar heavy thudding footsteps of the creature in the distance. His stomach had instantly turned to ice, but after a moment of stillness, he decided it was just his mind playing tricks on him.

At yet another branch in the passage he had been following, he had just selected the one to take and was heading toward it when he heard the unmistakable scream of Christina, instantly sending his stomach plummeting and his heart into a freefall.

Chapter Thirty-Three
Christina

Still shaky and reeling from the horrific sight of her best friend's mangled remains, Christina stumbled through the passage, desperately trying to banish the gruesome image from her mind as she focused on Mason.

Loose rocks choked the path, slowing her progress as she carefully picked her way around them, testing her already unsteady balance. Having lost Sarah, Adam, and Jenny, there was only she, Mason, and Jack left now. That was if Jack and Mason were even still alive. Had Jack been with Sarah and Mason? She recalled Sarah's discarded clothes she had found in the lake cavern. There was no way Sarah and Mason would have gone skinny dipping with Jack there. So, where was Jack? Had he found another passage to follow? Or was he...? She didn't even want to consider that option. She had already lost Sarah. She couldn't cope with losing Jack, too. A knot of apprehension tightened in her stomach as worry coursed through her. Her mind pictured all sorts of terrible ways Jack could have met his end. Christina's heart ached with the weight of her fear and grief. It was all too much to bear, but she had to keep going.

Taking a few deep breaths, Christina pressed on. She had to believe that Jack was still out there, and she wouldn't stop until she found him. In the meantime, her priority was finding Mason.

Her steps steadied as she regained her focus. A few minutes later, her flashlight caught a glimpse of something unusual—a small alcove hidden within the shadows. Her curiosity piqued, Christina approached, stopping at the mouth of the opening. The beam of her flashlight revealed a chilling sight: the skeletal remains of a miner, slumped against the back wall of the alcove. An abandoned pickaxe lay nearby, its handle worn and splintered with age, the head rusty.

Christina's breath caught in her throat as she took in the scene. The miner's bones were bleached white, standing out amongst the dark, damp rock surrounding them. Tattered remnants of old clothing clung to the skeleton. They had clearly been here for decades.

The sight, as confronting as it was, also began to give her a slight boost of hope. If the miner had found a way down here, then there had to be a way out. Thinking of the creature that was in pursuit of Mason, she approached the pickaxe and knelt to examine it further. As rusty, worn, and splintered as it was, it still looked like it might be usable. She reached for it and grasped it by the handle, hefting it off the ground. It was heavy, and the handle shifted slightly as she lifted it, but it held together. If she were lucky, it might be good for one swing before it disintegrated. She would just have to make it count if it came to that.

Up until now, she had been carrying her backpack in one hand and the flashlight in the other. Now she had no choice but to sling her backpack over her shoulder. She did so slowly and let out a gasp as sharp pangs of pain shot down through her shoulder and back where the backpack made contact with her bandaged wound. Grimacing, she endured the burning pain, knowing the weapon was worth the agony.

She gave a final, respectful glance at the miner's remains.

"Rest in peace," she whispered, her voice barely audible. "Thanks for giving me hope again."

She turned back toward the passage and headed down it with a renewed sense of determination. The cave seemed to close in around her, but she pressed on, driven by the desperate hope that she wasn't too late for Mason and the urgent need to find Jack.

Every step was painful, but it meant nothing now in the face of the bigger picture. Ahead, she saw the passage ending and a wide black expanse beyond. Reaching it, she stood in awe of the spectacle of the gigantic cavern she found herself at the lip of. Directly ahead of her were huge stalagmites, covering the floor as far as her torchlight would allow. Clusters of stalactites littered the ceiling, illuminated faintly by the glow of minerals.

As she directed the beam of light to inspect the stalactites above, a flurry of movement caught her eye. A group of bats, disturbed by the sudden brightness, took to the air in a chaotic flurry with angry shrieks. Their wings beat rapidly, creating a soft, rustling sound that echoed through the cavern. Christina watched in amazement as the bats darted and swooped, seeking refuge from the intensity of the light in the darker recesses of the cave.

Her chest tightened, both from the unexpected sight and the terror it evoked. She was reminded of what the bats had turned Jenny into and her own close call, and these looked like the same type. The bats moved like shadows, their silhouettes flickering against the rocky walls. Tension drained from Christina's body as the last of the bats disappeared into the darkness, leaving the cavern silent once more.

Other than the colony of stalagmites ahead, small patches of illuminated moss and the glitter of minerals in remote areas showed just how huge the cavern was. It would be a massive task to find Mason in here if he went anywhere other than straight ahead.

She mulled over what to do briefly before deciding on a straight course. If Mason had been running from the creature, then he most likely would have favoured that option. Although in his panic, he could have really done anything. Still, she decided to try her luck. If she didn't find anything, she would begin her search of the rest of the vast space.

She set her sight on the stalagmites, steadying herself before she made her way toward them. Her footsteps squelched on the guano-covered ground as soon as she entered the cavern. The air rose around her with a musky scent, tinged with a hint of ammonia, and she shuddered in disgust, her eyes watering as she lifted the bottom of her shirt to cover her nose. She scanned the tops of the glittering stalagmites as she went, in case there was a stray bat or two that dared to brave the bright glow of her flashlight, but the way thankfully remained clear.

As she rounded the last of the stone spires, she was presented with an open expanse in front of her. In the distance, she could see the ground slope upwards into a hill of some sort. To its right, the path remained clear. She decided to avoid the hill. Up was the opposite direction that she wanted to head in. The ground turned from the mushy wetness of the guano back to the hardened rock she was used to. Above her, out of sight of her flashlight, she could hear the occasional cry of a bat obviously angered at her presence but unwilling to dare the bright light. She silently thanked her foresight in going back and getting a fresh flashlight. If she had stuck with her almost flat one, she felt sure those things would've swarmed her and possibly afflicted her with the same thing they had given Jenny. That thought made her skin crawl. She was thankful that the one that had attacked her in the gap had only gotten caught in her hair and left her otherwise unharmed.

She veered off course slightly when the ground began to slope upwards and continued her journey to reach the other side. So far, there had been no sign of Mason. It had been some time now since she had heard his cry. The more she thought about it, the more she began to doubt it was him at all, but she was certain he had come this way all the same. There was no other option left to him. If it wasn't for her injury, she would have gotten here far sooner to try to back him up. Her stop at the small alcove didn't help, but she needed a weapon if she was to face that creature.

The cave wall began to loom in front of her, and she scanned it as she walked, looking for some sign of where Mason could have gone. There was nothing obvious in her immediate vicinity, so she stopped for a moment to think. If Mason had kept running in a straight line from the exit, he would have gone up the incline she had passed by. She turned back to face it and walked in that direction. There were more signs of bats in that area, their occasional angry shrieks emanating from that direction. Reaching the top of the hill, she saw the ground fall away sharply; the slope down was far steeper and covered in loose scree. It looked like there had been a landslide of some sort recently, judging by how loose and scattered the rocks were on that side. With a frown, she followed the rocks' path with her flashlight. There was a hollow tucked away in one area of the nearby wall. She decided to take a quick look just in case he had ended up there, if he had taken a tumble down the slope.

A few moments later, she was at the entrance, peering in to check for any evidence of Mason. Near the back wall, she spotted a few drops of blood, which sent her concern skyrocketing. Had Mason been injured in the fall? Given how steep the slope was, she wouldn't have been surprised. The blood was too fresh to have been there long, so Mason's departure must have been recent.

Exiting the hollow, she scanned along the cave wall and found what she was looking for further down, another passage. She approached it with a pained wince, her teeth clenched tight. She felt the strain of her journey heavily on her back now. Despite the bandaging, it felt like each movement and bump of the backpack was tearing her wound open anew.

She entered the passage, straining her ears for any sign of Mason ahead. There had been no sign of the creature either, and that made her nervous. If it had caught sight of Mason and if he was injured, it would no doubt catch up to him quickly.

There were too many ifs to think about. She forced herself to concentrate on what was in front of her. Thinking about anything else would turn her into a nervous wreck.

The passage split into two ahead, one narrow and one larger but sloping downward. The sight of the narrow passage brought back traumatic memories of the gap she had gotten stuck in. There was no way she was going to chance it this time, not with her back in the condition it was in.

She elected to take the larger passage and headed into it. Despite the steep slope and the loose gravel threatening to send her tumbling, she managed to keep her footing. The passage seemed to stretch on forever as she ventured deeper. She moved cautiously, each step deliberate, as the path meandered like a serpent through the bowels of the earth.

Time seemed to stretch, the minutes blending into an endless march through the twisting, turning corridor. Christina's legs ached from the constant descent, adding to the pain of her back. Her arms begged her to release the pickaxe she still held, but she resisted the impulse and forced herself onward.

After what felt like an eternity, the passage began to level out, then gradually climb upward. As committed as she was to finding Mason, she couldn't help but feel a glimmer of hope sparking within her at the thought of this passage leading her toward the surface.

Before her, the slope began to even out once more as a faint blue luminous light came into view. Christina's breath caught in her throat as she emerged from the passage into a cavern. A few meters away, a massive rock formation cast a deep shadow over where she stood. Beyond it, she saw the welcoming soft light of countless glowworms illuminating the walls and ceiling, their tiny lights twinkling like a galaxy above her. Her look of initial wonder soon gave way to horror when she saw a twisted, mangled figure lying motionless on the ground. It was Mason, or what was left of him. His body was shredded, torn apart by what could only have been that creature Jenny had become. Vast pools of blood surrounded him; more blood than seemed possible for a human body to hold.

Christina's knees buckled, and she fell to the ground with a shrill, piercing scream filled with terror and loss, her flashlight and pickaxe clattering beside her. She couldn't tear her eyes away from the gruesome sight. Mason's face was barely recognizable, his eyes mercifully closed, but his expression twisted in untold pain and suffering. The sight was a nightmare come to life, a vision of horror that, along with her recollection of Sarah and Adam's bodies, would haunt her forever.

Tears streamed down her cheeks as she reached out a trembling hand, her fingers brushing against Mason's torn clothing. "Mason," she breathed, her voice catching in her throat, a choked whisper barely audible. "I'm so sorry."

The cavern seemed to tighten like a clenched fist around her, the darkness pressing down like a suffocating shroud. She felt a wave of nausea as her gut churned with grief and fear. Once again, her stomach heaved, evacuating the last of what it had left onto the ground.

She gasped for air, grief coiling around her like an unrelenting current.

It felt like she was on the brink of a breakdown, but she couldn't allow that to happen. Jack was still out there, somewhere in this hellish cave system. She had to find him, had to save him from whatever had done this to Mason, or try to at least. She recalled her mother's voice, soft and calming, guiding her through the breathing exercises that always pulled her back from losing it completely. Tears blurring her vision, she stumbled through several failed attempts before finally finding the familiar pattern that had helped her countless times.

A few minutes later, with one last deep, shuddering breath, Christina picked up both flashlight and pickaxe and forced herself to stand, her legs shaking beneath her.

She tore her eyes away from the horrifying scene in front of her and swung her flashlight around to examine the area. The rock formation she had emerged into the cavern behind appeared more like an altar of some sort from where she now stood, a massive stone structure that seemed to rise from the ground like a monument to some ancient forgotten deity. Dried, crusted bloodstains told a story of what could only have been sacrifices or offerings. An open hole in the cave roof above, its rim similarly smeared with aged blood seemed to confirm her suspicions. The sight confused her at first, but then a terrifying question crossed her mind. What if there were other creatures like Jenny in here? It was entirely possible, especially if other people had encountered the bats and gotten infected like Jenny had.

Her thoughts were put on hold when she caught sight of another entrance to a passage beyond the altar. Above it, her torchlight caught the metallic glint of a rusted sign, clearly placed there by human hand. As traumatized as she was, she felt a flicker of hope. But with that hope came a gnawing fear. The rusted sign was a relic of the past, a silent witness to the dangers that lurked within the cave. What had happened to those who had left it there? Had they met the same fate as the skeleton she had found, or had they found their way out?

She began to approach the entrance when she heard a voice behind her that stopped her in her tracks.

"Christina?"

It was an unmistakable voice, brimming with both urgency and relief. Tears welled in her eyes, and with a choked sob, she turned around. Standing there at the entrance to a passage she hadn't noticed before was a ragged-looking and weary Jack.

CHAPTER THIRTY-FOUR
JACK

Jack raced through the passage, Christina's scream still echoing in his head. Knowing how the cave played tricks with sound, he wasn't sure if she was close or far away. As he came to a branch ahead, he chose the one that he thought the sound had come from and found it sloping upwards slightly. He came up on another branch, and he stopped in frustration. He dearly wanted to yell out to Christina, but he knew at least one of the creatures was in the tunnels, and he didn't want to attract its attention. Although maybe it had already caught up to her and was the cause of the scream. But if it wasn't and he was close by, it could draw the creature not only to him but to her as well.

"Fuck!" he whispered to himself. Left or right? Panic clawed at his mind, threatening to overwhelm him. Closing his eyes for a moment, he tried to steady his racing thoughts. He had to find her. He couldn't let fear paralyze him now. He went with his instincts and chose the right passage, his legs pumping with each stride.

A glow appeared ahead, and he increased his speed, his

heart pounding as sweat dripped down his forehead and stung his eyes. As the light intensified, he paused at the tunnel's end, gazing upon a horrifying yet joyful sight.

Blood covered the cavern floor from a ravaged body that was undeniably Mason's. Beyond that, at the other end of the cavern and on her way towards another passage, was Christina.

"Christina?" he called out, a jumble of emotions colouring his voice.

Christina spun around, her eyes locking with his, a cry of joy and relief bursting forth from her lips.

"J... Jack? Is that really you? I'm not hallucinating, am I?" she said, taking a few hesitant steps toward him.

"Yes, babe, it's really me."

Dodging the shattered remains of Mason, he ran to her, his heart hammering, pulling her into a desperate embrace. Her backpack hit the ground with a dull thump, the pickaxe falling with a metallic clang next to it, as her head fell against the warmth of his chest.

"Oh, god, Jack, I..." she began, but broke down in tears. Her body trembled against his, her knees threatening to give way. He held her close with steady arms, his grip firm, yet careful, mindful of the injury to her back. He anchored her, solid and unwavering, being the rock she clearly needed him to be.

"Hey, shhhhh... It's ok. We'll be ok," he murmured, rocking her gently back and forth, his hands caressing her hair, filling each stroke with tenderness, love, and reassurance.

"But the others, they're... they're..."

"I'm sure they're ok. They're probably just lost somewhere. This place is a damn maze," he said, tears beginning to form in his own eyes as he stared at the ruined body of his best friend.

"No, you're not listening! They're dead, Jack, dead!"

Christina pushed away from him and hammered at his chest with weak blows of her fists. Jack stared at her, momentarily stunned by her unexpected words and sharp reaction.

"Hey... Hey... Come here," he said, wrapping her in his arms again, but this time her body was stiff and resistant against his.

"What do you mean? What happened?"

She stepped back out of his arms and turned away, facing in the direction of the exit.

"You killed them, that's what happened. Adam and Sarah are dead. Jenny is a fucking monster and Mason is... Well, you can see what happened to Mason. It's all your goddamn fault. If you had told someone we were here. If you had gone ahead and applied for that fucking permit and got rejected, we wouldn't be in this mess."

Her words hit him hard; shocked, he stumbled back to the cave wall.

"No... No... That can't be, what do you... Adam, Sarah... They're dead? How? What happened to Jenny?"

Sighing, Christina's shoulders drooped a little, but she remained stiff as she faced him. "Listen, can we get going before this thing comes back for us?" Not waiting for an answer, she grabbed her backpack and pickaxe and walked into the passage before she stopped and turned grudgingly. "I'll fill you in on the way."

She turned her back on him and walked on.

The emotions of shock, guilt, shame, and horror pressed down on Jack like a physical weight, his heart pounding a suffocating rhythm in his chest. Mason, and now Sarah and Adam too? How could this have happened? How could things have gone so wrong? All he wanted was to hang out with those closest to him and have some fun.

And Jenny had turned into a creature? Was that the one that chased Mason? How many of these fucking things were there?

His mind cycled these questions over and over. When he finally became aware of the outside world, he saw the glow of Christina's flashlight fade into the distance as she turned a corner.

Pushing himself off the wall, he walked on weak legs down the passage to follow her. His torchlight was fading fast, but he wouldn't need it for long after he caught up to Christina.

He jogged to try to catch up, each step filled with weariness and the weight of the deaths of his friends. Up ahead, he could see the passage widen and open out into another cavern. The glow of Christina's flashlight was sweeping the surrounding area in rapid, jerky movements.

"Babe, what's going on? Is everything all right?"

"Does it look like everything's all right to you?" she snapped, shaking the hand that held the flashlight, directing him where to look.

"Holy shit," Jack managed as he looked upon the area the pool of light illuminated.

To the side of the passage he had entered, a deep pit had been dug into the bottom of the cave, and it was filled to ground level with bones, half-intact skeletons, tattered clothing, miners' helmets, and other ancient equipment. He stared into the pit, the sight of what lay before him so nightmarish that it stole the air from his lungs. Most of the bones were yellowed with age, brittle, and covered in a fine layer of dust. But among them, Jack noticed a few that looked disturbingly fresh, their stark whiteness standing out against the older remains.

The air was thick with the scent of decay and damp

earth. The smell, coupled with what he was seeing, made him queasy.

He crouched down by the edge of the pit and reached out a trembling arm, picking up a miner's helmet. He studied its pitted, corroded surface. The weight of it in his hand felt like a connection to the past, a tangible link to the lives that had been lost here.

"They did this? The fucking creatures did this?"

"Creatures? What do you mean creatures? Don't tell me there's more than just one."

Christina's voice was strained with panic. Reflected in the torchlight, her face appeared pale, almost as white as the bones themselves.

"Babe, we should probably keep going. You know, just in case those things are still nearby," Jack said, shifting nervously.

"No, Jack, I need to know, just tell me," Christina demanded, her chest heaving as if she were about to start hyperventilating.

Jack sighed and nodded. He would just have to keep an ear out for signs of the things while he tried to fill Christina in. Not the best time to be doing it, but it was clear Christina wasn't thinking rationally right now.

"Babe, I'm sorry to tell you this, but yeah, there's more than one. One of them has been following me, even toying with me, since I got through the gap. You know the giant cavern you had to go through to get here?" he asked as he placed the miner's helmet respectfully back on the bone pile.

"Ye... Yeah?"

"I saw Mason when I first arrived there. I'd just come out of a passage somewhere high above the cavern. There were the remains of an old bridge in front of me, but it was destroyed, so I couldn't cross. The fucking bat thing was behind me. Then I heard the flap of wings approaching and saw another one of the things coming toward me. I thought I was done for. That was when I saw Mason, down on the ground. He was jumping, screaming, and waving to try to draw the flying thing away from me, trying to buy me some time, and it worked. He ran, and the flying thing followed him into a passage. I looked for a way down and managed to find one, and somehow lost the creature behind me. But by the time I reached the floor and followed them, they were gone."

"Oh, Jesus, Jack," she said, her voice wavering in fear. "I think that thing that followed Mason... that was flying toward you, was Jenny."

"What happened, sweetheart?" he asked gently.

Christina blew out a breath, trying to steady her voice. "When you guys left, we all fell asleep. Adam woke up sometime later and went to check on Jenny. She... She wasn't doing so well, feverish and shaking. Adam went to retrieve the backpacks from the entrance, and I fell asleep again. When I woke up, she... She was..."

She began to sob once again, and Jack walked toward her and wrapped her in his arms. This time, there was no resistance. She dropped her backpack and pickaxe and clung to him, her body trembling as she fought for breath through her tears. Beyond her, he could see a passage near the end of the cavern, but he put that aside for the moment to focus on Christina.

A few moments later, she released him, and Jack took her hands, holding them so she knew he was there for her as she continued.

"She was making these strange sounds, snuffling, growling, gurgling as if she were struggling for breath, but she didn't sound human. Adam came back and ran to her, and she... she changed... Oh god, she changed before our eyes into that thing... that creature, whatever the fuck it is, it wasn't Jenny anymore, it was a monster. It attacked Adam and it... it... tore him apart."

She stopped, her body shaking with heavy sobs, tears falling onto the ground below.

"I managed to escape through the gap, but the thing... It burst through the wall as if it were paper. I hid, and it went by me, down a tunnel which I was about to head into. I waited until it was gone, then went in after it. I didn't want it to catch you or Mason and Sarah. The passage led to a cavern with a lake, and I found..." She gulped, trying to contain her sobs but failing. Jack gave her hands a squeeze, and she looked up at him tearfully, her eyes full of unrestrained pain and anguish. "Sarah... There was only her lower half left, floating in the water. She's gone, Jack, I can't believe she's gone, my best friend..."

She staggered into his arms, and he embraced her as she poured out her tears of heartbreak and loss. His own tears fell freely and silently. The pain and loss he felt were unimaginable, but he knew it would be worse for Christina. Guilt, shame, and grief tore through him in waves, but he couldn't allow himself to give in. Not now, not when there was hope for them to get out. He held her until her tears began to abate and her trembles lessened, his mind set now on the task ahead. There was nothing that would stop him from getting Christina out of there, even if it was the last thing he did.

He released his embrace, placing his hands gently on her shoulders as he stepped back to gaze into her eyes.

"Hey, listen. I won't let anything happen to you, you hear me? We're going to get out of here. We're so close now, I can feel it."

She looked at him, tears still glistening in the corners of

her eyes, a semblance of hope flickering through them at his words. She nodded hesitantly.

Gently, with his thumbs, he wiped away her tears, then kissed her forehead softly. "I love you, babe. So, so much." With a final, tender embrace, he poured all the love in his heart into the moment, holding her close before letting her go. "Let's get out of here, hey? But first, let me chuck all our stuff into one backpack, and I'll carry it and the pickaxe. You've gone through enough pain, no need to go through more."

She nodded with a ghost of a smile on her pale, weary face. She walked over towards the pit of bones as he went about reorganizing the contents of the backpacks.

He heard the clatter of bones and metal behind him as he worked. A few minutes later, he was done and stood up to strap the backpack over his shoulders, and grabbed the pickaxe from the ground. He turned toward Christina, who had an old hammer in her hand, examining it with her flashlight.

"Nice find," he said with a smile. "Looks in pretty good condition, too. Ready to go?"

She nodded once more. Her face was drawn and haggard, etched with worry lines and exhaustion.

Putting aside his concern for her appearance, he smiled and reached toward her for the flashlight. "Here, let me take that."

"No, it's ok. You're going to need your hands for the pickaxe if we come across those creatures."

He hesitated, then nodded reluctantly. "Ok, but stay close to me, yeah?"

She gave him a nod and turned to face the passage he had seen earlier. As they got closer, he could see it had a sharp incline. It was going to be a challenge to navigate, but they would have to manage.

She entered before him, hammer at the ready, and Jack followed close behind, pickaxe held in both hands.

Although steep, the upward slope of the passage was manageable, though arduous for both of them. Its walls narrowed as they ascended, funnelling them toward the unknown. Jack had to steady Christina at points when her feet slipped under loose rock, but they pushed on. Gradually, the tunnel began to even out, and they paused for a moment to catch their breath.

Afterwards, they continued on and came upon some peculiar structures jutting out from the walls—mineral formations that stretched out like the tendrils of some ancient, subterranean plant, their slender forms winding and curling in every direction. Some spiralled gracefully, their delicate tips reaching out into the tunnel, while others branched off into multiple, gnarled paths, creating a web of stone that seemed almost alive. The mineral deposits that formed them glistened in the light, giving the formations a crystalline sheen that added to their allure.

"This place never ceases to amaze me," Jack said, running his fingers over one of the shapes, feeling flecks of crystal flake off as he did.

"Those are helictites if I remember correctly. It's like a whole other world down here. It would be beautiful if it weren't for, you know, the giant fucking monsters trying to kill us," Christina agreed.

"Come on, let's get out of here. I'm over this place, despite its beauty."

She moved forward with Jack shadowing her, twisting and turning to avoid the outcroppings that continued to emerge in front of them. As they wound their way through the last of the strange formations, the passage opened up in front of them. They emerged into another large cavern, this one giving an indication as to how close they must now be to the surface.

Christina's flashlight parted the darkness to reveal another natural wonder. Gnarled and twisted roots from trees that must lie directly above them glistened in the light as water droplets fell from them into shimmering water puddles beneath, creating a soothing, melodic echo. The floor of the cavern was uneven, giving the water a place to form small pools.

Another passage lay on the opposite side of the cavern, this one continuing the trend upwards to what surely had to be the exit.

"That has to be it, babe. We're almost there," Jack said, his words laced with nervous excitement and a glimmer of hope. "C'mon, let's go!" he said, walking confidently toward the passage. He stepped around the puddles, choosing his path carefully as Christina followed behind, illuminating his path forward.

"Wait, Jack, I can't walk as fast as you."

"Sorry, babe, I..."

A sudden movement caught his eye. From the shadows of an alcove he hadn't spotted, one of the creatures lunged at him, its form a blur of limbs and wings.

Jack only just had time to react. The brute's eyes glowed with a malevolent yellow light, and its jaws snapped open, revealing rows of sharp, jagged teeth. It moved with terrifying speed. Jack stumbled backward, his heart racing as he raised his pickaxe in a desperate attempt to fend off the attack. The creature threw itself sideways at the last second, narrowly avoiding the head of the raised pickaxe. It spun around and hissed before launching itself toward him once more. This time, Jack managed to dodge the thing's talons, scraping against the rock where he had stood moments before. He swung the pickaxe, and the creature recoiled, its lightning reflexes saving it at the last moment, giving Jack a precious few seconds to regain his footing.

Adrenaline surged through him as he backed away, trying to buy some time to come up with a plan. Christina screamed in terror as the creature circled him. Its movements were fluid and predatory, its eyes fixed only on him. Jack knew he had to act quickly. He backed off, trying to keep himself between the monster and Christina.

The creature lunged toward him, but this time, Jack read its body movements and was ready. He swung the pickaxe with all his might, sending a shockwave up his arms as the head impacted with its body and embedded itself within, the handle snapping off with a loud crack. The creature let out a pained screech and staggered backwards. It stared down at the foreign object embedded deep into its side before it raised its head to stare at him, snarling in anger. The light of Christina's flashlight wobbled unsteadily as it fixed on the monstrosity, drawing its attention.

"What the fuck do I have to do to kill you?" Jack shouted, trying to draw its gaze back toward him. He took a tentative step forward. The creature's eyes flickered towards him, then back to Christina, its focus lingering on her. It began to stumble toward her, clearly weakened but not enough to deter it from the walking fresh meat in front of it.

"Oh, no you don't, you son of a bitch!" Jack yelled as he ran towards the creature at full tilt.

"Jack, no!" Christina screamed behind him, but he was fully committed. There was no way he was going to let this thing get anywhere near her.

The beast backpedalled in surprise, extending its wings to take flight, but Jack was quicker. He slammed into the creature shoulder first and drove it to the ground, Jack's added body weight on top of it, adding to the impact. The thing thrashed beneath him, screeching in pain as Jack straddled its waist, trying to grab hold of the axe head and push it in deeper. Just as he had a hand on it, the creature swung an arm at him, talons extended, and raked him across his chest, tearing through his shirt as if it were paper and gouging deep scratches in his flesh.

White hot pain ripped through Jack, and he fell sideways, blood spilling between the fingers of his frantically clutching hands.

The creature took advantage, and it scrambled to get up, raising itself above him. Jack swung a fist at it, connecting with its head, but it hardly flinched at the impact. It looked at him, exposing its teeth and hissing, as it raised its arm and swung. Jack rolled at the last second but still felt the sharp, knifelike extensions slicing deep into his chest, above the breastbone.

He screamed, a ragged, guttural sound of pure agony, the world blurring into darkness at his vision's edges. As Jack watched the creature's silhouette poised for another attack above him, the sickening thud of metal on flesh echoed from behind it. It hesitated, a confused look in its eyes, then came another thud, and another after that.

"Get the fuck off him!" Christina screamed, her form just visible behind the creature in Jack's blurred vision. The monster emitted an ear-piercing shriek and swung an arm backwards, connecting with her head with a loud crunch. The hammer fell to the ground along with the flashlight as she fell backwards with a strangled cry. The creature wheeled around to face her as another screech, this time one of pure rage, tore from its throat.

"Christina!" Jack tried to call out, but his voice was barely a whisper. Jack's heart pounded in his chest, a surge of adrenaline momentarily pushing back the pain. He knew he had to act, do something to save her. Summoning every ounce of strength he had left, he rolled to his side and extended an arm towards the fallen hammer. His fingers brushed against the handle, and with a final, desperate effort, he grasped it tightly. The creature turned its attention to him, its eyes narrowing as it sensed the threat.

A wave of dizziness washed over Jack, and the beast seemed to split into two hazy, wavering forms in his darkened vision.

"C'mon, you prick," he managed weakly.

His voice was enough to spur the brute into action, and it leapt toward him. Jack swung the hammer with all his remaining strength. The blow impacted its head with a brutal crack, splintering the compromised bone left from Christina's previous attack and digging into the soft brain matter within. The creature let out a shriek of pain as it reeled back. Its jaw snapped open and shut, as its sightless eyes bulged out of its sockets. After a few more feeble, instinctive beats of its wings, it crumpled lifelessly onto the ground.

Jack let the hammer slip from his grasp, the last of his strength spent. He looked at Christina, who had regained her feet and was approaching him, sobbing. Her figure flickered in and out of his vision, a teasing dance of light and shadow, and he smiled.

"You're safe now," he whispered, his voice barely audible. "I love you."

As the world faded to black, Jack felt a sense of peace. He had saved her, and that was all that mattered.

CHAPTER THIRTY-FIVE
CHRISTINA

Christina knelt beside Jack and sobbed as she ran her trembling fingers over his eyelids gently to close them one final time. Tears continued to stream down her face as she leaned forward and kissed him on the lips. Her heart was shattered, her world forever changed. She'd lost her soulmate, the one she thought she would end up growing old with; not only that, but all those closest to her besides family.

Family. She still had that. Her loving sister, who adored and worshipped her. Her mother and father, who she was blessed to have supporting her. A loving home to return to. She would need them now more than ever. She had lost everything else.

Looking down at Jack one last time, she kissed him on the forehead and brushed his hair back into place on his fast-cooling and clammy skin. Their moments together—the laughter, the shared dreams, the quiet moments of comfort and love. All of it had been ripped away from her in just a matter of minutes, leaving her with an unbearable emptiness. But even in her grief, she knew that Jack had given everything to protect her. That his love had been a beacon of light in the darkness.

"I love you, too," she whispered softly. "I swear I'll come back for you and give you the burial you deserve."

She tore herself away from him and stood up, utterly drained both physically and mentally, but she still needed to get out of here. To make Jack's sacrifice worth something.

She picked up her flashlight, which had miraculously avoided being damaged in the scuffle, and left the backpack underneath Jack where it lay.

The walk was torturous, every step laden with the weight of her grief and memories that would haunt her forever. A few minutes later, she was making her way through the passage. The uneven floor showed signs of a coating of dirt beneath, and Christina knew she was close to the exit.

As she rounded the bend, a warm orange-red light filled the passage, yet her joy at nearing freedom felt muted, almost numb by the events she had been through.

As she stepped out of the cave, the cool, fresh air hit her face, a stark contrast to the damp, musty atmosphere she had endured for hours. She paused for a moment, closing her eyes and taking a deep breath, filling her lungs with the scent of pine and earth. The sky was alight with the burgeoning colors of dawn, shades of honey and peach blending seamlessly with the fading night.

She had emerged onto a cliff face. A narrow trail extended from the ledge, around the corner of the mountain, toward a sparse-looking forest. She walked along the ledge and made it onto the ground, where her legs promptly gave way, and she sank to her knees. She lifted her face to the sun, letting its gentle rays warm her before reaching into her pocket for her phone. It was on 5%, just enough to call home.

Chapter Thirty-Six

The creature settled into the alcove, feeling the new life blossoming inside of her. She had felt keenly the loss of the male as the presence of the humans, the ones she was curiously familiar with, departed. Only one had left, leaving behind enough meat to sustain her until she was ready to give birth to her offspring. It wouldn't be long now; she could feel it. Her smaller cousins gathered around her, forming a protective barrier to anything that might threaten her. Though they bore the same blood, they were primitive, incapable of rational thought. Despite that, they still had their uses. They had helped create her after all.

She gazed at the bodies before her. Once she had left the male, she had been busy gathering the food sources from where they had lain in death. Her first victim upon transformation, the one she and the male had killed together, and the one that had killed the male, all on the ground beneath her. She had left the remains of the body in the water for the creature from the lake. Even she would not dare to encroach upon its territory. She would engorge herself on them before the meat went bad, her body storing it away within to sustain her during the gestation period.

Where once there was but one male, soon her species would flourish with new blood. The thought filled her with a dark satisfaction, a sense of purpose for her monstrous existence. She would bring forth a new generation, and they would thrive in the shadows, their legacy written in the blood of those they would soon spill.

Acknowledgments

A book, although written alone, isn't released (or at least shouldn't be) without the help of others who make it better. *Unholy Blood* is no exception. Huge thanks go to Stephanie Huddle, my editor, for catching all the things I missed during self-editing. Grammar issues, and comma placements, aside, she caught me out on several factual errors, and continuity issues, that I'll be forever grateful for.

Thanks also to Adrian Medina, for the brilliant, eye-catching cover. He is truly a gifted designer, and I'd highly recommend him for any cover—premade, or custom—you may need. To my formatter, Jyl Glenn, for putting this book together, and for your friendship. Speaking of which, thanks also to the Scribe group I am lucky to be involved with. Your support, friendship, and help with things in, and out of the book world, means more to me than you'll know.

Before *Unholy Blood*, came *Saving Tommy*, and that one being my first release, it totally slipped my mind to include acknowledgements. Call it a novice mistake.

I need to thank Savannah Fischer for the amazing cover for *Saving Tommy*, and her patience with all the changes, and ideas I kept throwing at her. Thanks also for your friendship, and support. For my editor on that one, Marked Up Editing—another brilliant editor, which I'd highly recommend. The ending wouldn't have been the same without your input. And once again, thanks to Jyl Glenn, for the formatting.

Finally, to my wonderful partner, Misty. Thanks for listening to my horrifying ideas, even though horror isn't your genre. I hope I haven't given you nightmares!

About the Author

A horror fan since childhood, Ian embraces his inner geek with pride, his dedication displayed in the intimidating collection of horror novels and video games that threaten to take over his living space.

He is mad for all things Alien, Star Wars, and cats, his furry companions always there to keep him company as he scribbles down his latest ideas.

He's a father in Melbourne, Australia, sharing his home with his partner, two stepdaughters, and four cats. The sheer number of furry and human companions in his life might be enough to drive anyone a little crazy.

You can follow his writing journey on Facebook at - Ian Gielen – Author

MORE FROM IAN GIELEN

Horror Novella:

Saving Tommy

Anthologies:

Devour the Rich (Published by Above the Rain Collective)

Cryptid Codex (Published by Crimson Cult Media)

Warning: Wicked Web (Published by Crimson Cult Media)

Invasion of the Saucer-Men from Mars! (Published by Specul8 Publishing)

Books of Horror Community Anthology Vol 4 Part 1 (Published by Books of Horror)

Petting Boo! (Published by Wicked Shadow Press)

Christmas of the Dead: Krampus Kountry (Published by Wicked Shadow Press)

Apocalyptales: Judgement Day (Published by Wicked Shadow Press)

Flash of the UnDead (Published by Wicked Shadow Press)

Flash of the Dead: Requiem (Published by Wicked Shadow Press)

Femme Fatale Flashes (Published by Wicked Shadow Press)

Masks of Sanity: The Monster Within (Published by Wicked Shadow Press)

Children of the Dead: Lost Lullabies (Published by Wicked Shadow Press)

Halloweenthology: Trick-Or-Treat (Published by Wicked Shadow Press)

Flash of the Dead: Halloween '24 (Published by Wicked Shadow Press)

Halloweenthology: Friar's Lantern (Published by Wicked Shadow Press)

Blink of an Eye (Published by CultureCult Magazine & Press)

Merry Creepsmas: The Green Book (Published by Wicked Shadow Press)

Cooks of Horror

Sleeve of Hearts

Coming Soon:

Echoes of the Damned (Collection)

Mother of Mine (Novel)

www.ingramcontent.com/pod-product-compliance
Lightning Source LLC
Chambersburg PA
CBHW070313190726
48291CB00012B/1142